*K*anika walked up to Tyrell and looked down at him as he sat on the plush, leather couch. "Does this look like the body of a little girl?" she asked, taking a drag from the cigar.

Tyrell licked his lips, soaked up her curves, and raised his eyebrows.

She blew the smoke in his face and straddled him with her legs. She sat on him, face to face, and touched a healed stab wound under his left jaw.

Tyrell maintained a serious demeanor, keeping his body relaxed and his hands to himself.

"Tyrell? You don't ever think about us? Or me? One day?" Kanika parted her lips and let them graze the edge of Tyrell's closed mouth. The softness of her lips invited him to taste. She took his hand and placed it on the voluptuous curve of her behind and pressed her breasts into him. Finally, he opened his mouth, and so did she, and they kissed hard, his tongue over-powering hers.

She reached down to touch below his belt, but he grabbed her hand and stopped her. He pushed her away.

"Whatsup?" Kanika said, confused and feeling silly for putting herself out there.

"Yo, chill wit all that, Kanika," he said, angrily. "I'm a grown man, little girl. I don't play games. And in my eyes, you will always be like my lil sista." He laughed, uncomfortably. "Besides, Tony said your mama ain't having it."

Kanika's suspicion was proven. Though her mother was encouraging her to holla at Tyrell because he was a "good catch," all the while Tony was putting salt in the game. She planned to have a little talk with her mother.

He glared at her, but when she stared back into his dark eyes, she saw that familiar softness behind them. It spoke what his mouth wouldn't. He wanted her despite his tough man talk, she thought. And she knew there was always next time . . .

Ghetto Princess

✦ ✦ ✦ ✦ ✦ ✦ ✦ ✦

Mia Edwards

St. Martin's Paperbacks

GHETTO PRINCESS

Copyright © 2006 by Mia Edwards.

Cover photo © Shirley Green

ISBN: 0-312-93875-6
EAN: 9780312-93875-8

Printed in the United States of America

St. Martin's Paperbacks edition / June 2006

St. Martin's Paperbacks are published by St. Martin's Press, 175 Fifth Avenue, New York, NY 10010.

10 9 8 7 6 5 4 3 2 1

One

"Mmmm, I wanna be the cream in the middle of that chocolate." Kanika soaked up all six feet, four inches of Tyrell standing at the other end of the bar.

"Girl, you know you can't even handle that grown-ass nigga. Plus, he roll wit' ya mama's man and you know he into some real shit out there," Peaches said as she slurped her drink. They watched Andre try to talk to two women standing near the dance floor. With the quickness they both dismissed him at the same time. Kanika and Peaches cracked up laughing.

"Andre couldn't catch a woman wit' a ten-million-dollar NBA contract." Kanika laughed as she watched her former classmate kick game to another girl against the wall at Crystal Palace. Tonight was a celebration of Kanika's mother, Waleema, and the "business" expansion of her man, Tony Black, who just took down his rival Cee-Lo and took over an extra $5 million in "work."

Kanika nodded her head to the beat and wrapped her long French-manicured nails around her glass of Henny and Coke. She was well aware of all the drama that had taken place in the streets the last few weeks, and though everyone seemed footloose and fancy-free, she was on-edge. She sipped her drink and gazed at her mother, who always seemed cool under pressure, even with a 9mm in her Chanel bag.

Waleema was only 105 pounds and five feet, four inches of rounded hips, a trim waist, melon-sized breasts, and cherry lips. Her Asian-shaped eyes gave her a sexy, mysterious look and disappeared when she smiled. With her black licorice skin, Waleema looked like an African China doll, dressed in a skin-tight black kimono-style minidress and her cornrow-braided hair cascading down her back. She sat on Tony's lap, momentarily rubbing his bald head as she chatted with a crew of her friends, mostly other "wives" of Tony's friends who looked up to her for her style, status, and the respect she enjoyed. Amid all the loud music and goings-on, everyone's attention was focused on Waleema's conversation as they laughed and egged her on while she told one of her many stories. But if Waleema was the queen, Kanika was the princess.

Only a few weeks away from turning eighteen, Kanika never felt more like her mother than she did now. As she watched Waleema entertain the grown folks, Kanika admired the way her mother worked a room. They both had the same features, too. Distinctive eyes, long "good hair," and bodacious frames, except Kanika was taller at five-seven. Tony and her mother's friends were always reminding her how she and Waleema looked alike. Sometimes people wondered why a woman like Waleema would be with a man like Tony. He wasn't that good-looking, fifty pounds overweight, with a glass eye from being shot when he was sixteen, a potbelly, and acne-prone skin at forty-two. He was five feet, five inches short but had more bank than the Federal Reserve. He treated Waleema well, too, hardly ever raising his voice at her, and keeping Kanika and Waleema safe out of harm's way. Tony had enough street cred, for coming up with some of the most notorious Harlem hustlers in the eighties, and now was the "head nigga in charge" during a time when the drug game was gasping its last breaths. But besides that, Kanika respected him as a father. His was the calming voice when she and her mother would go at it about Kanika's coming in late from school or a party. Sometimes, when her mother couldn't make some of her parent-teacher meetings, Tony would come dressed in one of his pin-striped Italian suits and have Kanika's female teachers swooning. She often wondered if he was the reason that she got preferential treatment. He wasn't a tall man, but he had a big presence when he walked into their home. Kanika understood that when Tony was around everything was all good.

She respected Tony most of all for taking her and her mother in when they had no place to go. After

Waleema had left Shon, Kanika's father, and traveled to New York City, they went from one friend's house to the next. Kanika remembered nights traveling against the cold, hard winter winds, kept warm by her mother's arms, when it was time for them to move on to the next place. Until one night Kanika remembered her mother leaving for a party with friends dressed in black and coming back in the morning dressed in white and gold. It wasn't too long before Tony took them into his four-family home in Bed-Stuy, Brooklyn. Since then, he had done everything for them. He sent clients and cash to Waleema's strip club, and she played the role of his "wifey," making sure his home was in order, his body satisfied, and his parties beautifully hosted.

Tonight was a celebration of Tony reaching the top of his game. Cee-Lo was gone, and that meant more money, more problems. But there was no time for stressin', as the Dom P. flowed as free as the bodies moving to the music in the lounge area. Top neighborhood ballers dropped Benjamins like hot potatoes on bottles of Cristal and the baddest girls and their friends. Waleema and Tony danced as Waleema showed off all her latest moves to a Jay-Z hit. Kanika and Peaches did the same when they took their champagne-filled glasses back to the dance floor.

The DJ spun one of Biggie's hits, "One More Chance," and Kanika flung her hand and her drink in the air to her favorite jam. Her shapely hips swayed from side to side as she and Peaches waved their glasses in the air with everyone else. Kanika was at her best this evening: she had her family and friends around her, her mother and Tony were looking happy, and she was about to graduate from high school any day. She couldn't think of anything else that would top this but a kiss from Tyrell. He was twenty-four and Tony's number-two man.

While she danced, Kanika kept her eye on him in case some other female tried to push up. Kanika had heard he was seeing some professional chick who used to roll with Cee-Lo or at least be his jump-off in between his baby mama drama. Kanika didn't know much about her, only that she was older and had a college degree and a good job at the bank. It was that job that helped Cee-Lo get loans to open his sneaker store and record label and hide his money in secret accounts. But she wasn't part of "the life" like Kanika was. Kanika was born in the game, like Tyrell, and if there was any woman who knew what Tyrell needed it was her. She remembered when Tony first brought him to the house. She had only been twelve and he had been eighteen. All she could remember was this tall, black, skinny guy with eyes so deep she could swim in them. Any time he walked by, her skin erupted in goose bumps. He didn't seem to pay her scrawny twelve-year-old frame any mind, but he teased her about her Asian-looking eyes, which she now understood meant he liked her even then. But they both had grown a lot since then. He was still over six feet, more muscular, and his dark, creamy black skin still made her want to lick him from head to toe.

"Girl, I can't believe high school is ova'. I am so tired of messing with those lil boys."

"Why are you so into older cats? They die soon, you know," Kanika said, bringing her hips down to the floor. She glanced at Tyrell, but there was a light-skinned, red-lipsticked woman on his arm. Kanika snapped back up. *It's that bitch.*

"Not that old. And any woman I see who got something got an older man. Look at your mama," Peaches said as they danced together.

Kanika tried to remember a time when Peaches was not talking about some older cat. Even when they were fourteen and in the eighth grade, she was checking for dudes out of high school. It was too much. But she knew it had a lot to do with the fact that Peaches' father left before she was born. Chick was looking for daddy in the face of every older cat she had ever gotten with. At least Kanika had Tony to fill that void. "Well, thank God you gonna be eighteen soon; then it can be legal."

"That kind of takes the fun out of it, but I'll live." Peaches' eyes stayed glued to one of Tyrell's older friends.

"Mine is only ten days away, and a bitch can't wait," Kanika said, as both of the girls laughed. But Kanika was fixed on Tyrell, as he stood all close to this girl.

"Excuse me," Kanika said abruptly, as she marched off the dance floor about to make her presence known to Tyrell.

"Uh-uh, where you think you going with that nasty look on your face?" Waleema asked as she stopped her daughter cold. Waleema gripped Kanika's shoulders. "You look like you about to go off. Something happen?"

Kanika didn't want to make a big deal. "I was just going to the bathroom."

Waleema followed Kanika's line of focus and smirked when her eyes landed on Tyrell. "Honey, don't tell me you about to go make a fool of yourself because a man is just being a man?"

Kanika tapped her foot impatiently as she cut her eyes away from Tyrell and his female companion. Waleema gently pulled her to a dark corner, away from the music and the noise. "I get a feeling that you got something more to say to Tyrell than hello. Am I right?"

Kanika ran her hands over her wavy black weave. "Mommy, I just wanted to say hello, but he's with that trick again," Kanika said, frustrated with herself. She had never gotten a chance to have a real conversation with Tyrell because he would always tease her about her being locked up because of her age. She wanted to show him that age was just a number when it came to her feelings for him.

"Baby, you gonna be eighteen soon. You gotta start acting more mature. You can't just storm over there and interrupt the man just because. You gotta do that with class, honey. Remember, a ho in the sheets and a princess in the streets. Understand?"

"I guess so," Kanika said, as she forced a smile. Her mother was never one to mince words. "So what do I do? I really like Tyrell and I know he's feeling me."

"He is, but be careful. If you want his attention, act like you don't care if he comes or goes. Don't you think he got enough women trying to get close to him? Be different. Walk right on by him," she said, emulating a sexy strut with her hands on her waist, "swinging those hips your mama gave ya, and don't take your eyes off him for one second." She spun around on her heels. "And get yourself a glass of the most expensive champagne at the bar," she said, handing Kanika a stack of bills.

Kanika stood alone as Tony swept her mother back up in his arms. She thought they looked cute, the way her mother stood taller than him in her four-inch gold Chanel stilettos. Kanika stuffed the money in her Prada bra and glided her way toward Tyrell. Her heart was in her mouth as she inched up closer to him. His back was against the bar and the chick was standing between his legs. As soon as Kanika turned the corner, Tyrell's eyes met hers. That gave her the extra confidence she needed; her skintight green and gold sequined Gucci dress did the rest. She pulled the V front down some to show off her cleavage. There were lots of people passing in front of her, but she made sure she followed her mama's rules. Kanika's eyes zeroed in on his face with a tempting look and a dash of attitude. *There were his deep brown eyes again.* In her mind, Kanika was already swimming in their depths. She was in a trancelike state, moving in slow motion with no one around but her and Tyrell. He was dressed in all-black linen slacks and shirt with a thick platinum chain and spinning hubcap pendant dangling from his neck. The strobe lights made his tea black skin radiate with a mysterious power that made him look good enough to jump. He diminished every other man in the room with his thick, muscular build and wide shoulders. His closely shaved head and beard made him look a few years older, with a handsome ruggedness. All Kanika could think of in those few seconds was sucking on his thick, brown lips. His gaze traveled from her breasts, to her hips, to her shapely legs as she glided right by him, careful not to even give his chick any recognition. Kanika slid into a space a few stools down and ordered her glass of champagne. Tyrell winked at her and smiled. The chick he was with turned his face toward her and Tyrell slapped her hand away.

Kanika snickered to herself. It was only a matter of time before she got Tyrell for herself, she thought. He always acted like she was too young for him, but she planned to show him soon that she could get as nasty as he wanted her to be.

Kanika walked back through the crowd to the dance floor, somewhat satisfied, to where Peaches was still carrying on with a group of other girls. "I can't wait to start college. As soon I get down to Atlanta, I'm gonna regulate on all dem prissy bitches," Peaches said out loud, and flung her weave to the other side of her face. "I'm gonna get me an older man, and take him for all his money."

Kanika laughed as they both got back into their groove with the others. "Where you disappear to?" Peaches asked.

"I just got me a little somethin' to wet my throat," Kanika said as she faced Peaches, who was working up a sweat.

"And your panties." She laughed. "I seen Tyrell over there, too."

Kanika rolled her eyes and laughed also. It was no secret how she felt about Tyrell; everyone knew, including Tony, who wasn't too crazy about them hooking up. Tyrell was what Tony called "a young cat" and too wild for his own good, but he kept him in his crew for those very reasons. He thought that Kanika was way too smart to be with a man who made his green on the streets, even if he was steep six figures. Kanika wondered if Tony had anything to do with Tyrell keeping his distance. But Tyrell was his own man. She couldn't imagine another man telling him who to date. And if her mother approved of him, Kanika thought, hooking up with him couldn't be so bad.

As the music changed to some eighties Prince and Cameo jams, Kanika wandered off the dance floor. When Kanika walked off, she noticed Peaches and a group behind her. It was a few of her classmates from school, but she wanted to be alone to find Tyrell. She turned around, looked at her diamond-studded Jacob the Jeweler watch, and said, "Listen, y'all can go and do your thang. I'm gonna chill for a few."

Peaches said, doing a fake karate stance, "If you need anything let me know, OK?"

"I will," Kanika said as they all walked away. She didn't know what she could possibly need. Somehow, girls liked hanging with her, because at school it brought them all the right attention from the right guys and made them look "cool." Little did they know that Kanika had her mind on bigger things than a school reputation. She had mastered school with good grades and exceptional performances as head of her cheerleading squad and school debate team. Her mother put heavy emphasis on studying, including a mandatory three hours of studying every Sunday. Sometimes Kanika had to find stuff to study, because she had already aced most of it. At this point, just days away from graduation, she was ready for life's bigger challenges.

Kanika slipped away from the party. She knew where to find Tyrell and she had to talk to him. She didn't understand why he was ignoring her all night, except for his little glances. She touched herself up in the women's bathroom and glossed her lips with cherry red color and dabbed her eyes with a touch of silver eyeliner. Her hair was still neatly styled, despite the heat and sweat.

She dabbed some Vaseline, a trick her mother had shown her, on the tops of her breasts to make her skin look dewy. Her mother had taught her to always accentuate what came natural. When Kanika left, a short brown-faced girl she had never seen before slipped her a note:

> *Tyrell is in the cigar room. Classy, sexy first.*
> *—Mommy*

Kanika tore the note up, adjusted her dress, and thanked God for a mother like hers. Sometimes she felt Waleema was more like a sister and that she wanted to see her with Tyrell more than anything. Perhaps Waleema knew how happy that would make Kanika, as Waleema was always looking for a way to please her.

Kanika walked into the cigar room just a few doors down from the ladies' room. She knew he had to be alone, but even if he wasn't, she was still going in. "Have you seen Peaches?" she said, slightly opening the door to the smoke-filled room. She could care less where Peaches was, but she had to play the game.

"Nah, her ass probably still out there dancing,"

Tyrell said, standing up and quickly opening a window. Her eyes fixated on his fat diamond T-initialed pinkie ring.

"Oh, OK," Kanika said, lingering by the door. She closed it behind her.

Tyrell put out his cigar and asked, "Keeping me company?"

"I just want a place to chill; it's kind of noisy out there," she said, leaning forward and sitting down.

Again she caught Tyrell's eyes on her breasts, but he looked away. She carefully crossed her legs, showing the curves of her healthy thighs. She sat across from him and waited.

"Yeah, I was saying that to myself. Too many fake motherfuckas out there," he said, sipping his glass of Henny. "Half them niggas I don't even know."

"They all our friends and Tony."

"Tony think he got friends now. Man, since that nigga Cee-Lo went down, all hell 'bout to break loose. Watch how many friends he gonna have in a few weeks."

"If you talking about Tony, you talking about all of us."

Tyrell shook his head like she didn't get it. "Listen, I just can't be relaxing when I know shit is hot out there right now with Cee-Lo gone. This ain't time for celebrating; heads about to roll."

Kanika was frightened by Tyrell's concern. He was also an intelligent person, and though she didn't admit it, she, too, was nervous when she first heard Cee-Lo was killed. But no one else seemed to care, like her mother and Tony. Everything seemed normal. "How you know all that? That chick you was talking to earlier?"

"Man," he said, lighting another cigar. "That trick may play dumb, but she knows a lot of shit. She told me that Cee-Lo's people ain't go down without a fight. Just because Cee-Lo gone don't mean a hundred motherfuckas is gone with him," he said, then laughed. "But their money sure is."

Tyrell passed the cigar to Kanika, who took a healthy pull. Tony had shown her how to smoke them just last year. She didn't like the taste, but she loved how she looked holding one between her fingers. As much as she wanted to believe Tyrell, she thought he was overreacting. Cee-Lo had been gone for weeks, and the streets were calm. Not too quiet, because that was when trouble was most suspected, but calm enough to know the winds had changed. Kanika wasn't too worried. "So who is this Cee-Lo chick? You fucking her?"

"Come on, Kanika. A grown-ass man like me," he said, flashing his handsome white smile, "is not gonna be explaining his sex life to a little girl."

Kanika walked over and looked down at him as he sat on the plush leather couch. "Does this look like the body of a little girl?" she asked, taking a drag from the cigar.

Tyrell licked his lips and marinated in her curves.

She blew the smoke in his face and straddled him with her legs. She sat on him, face-to-face, and touched a healed stab wound under his left jaw.

Tyrell maintained a serious demeanor, keeping his body relaxed and his hands to himself.

"Tyrell? You don't ever think about us? Or me? One day?" Kanika parted her lips and let them graze the edge of Tyrell's closed mouth. The softness of her lips invited him to taste. She took his hand and placed it on the voluptuous curve of her behind and pressed her breasts into his chest. Finally, he opened his mouth, and so did she, and they kissed hard, his tongue overpowering hers.

She reached down to touch below his belt, but he grabbed her hand and stopped her. He pushed her away.

"Whatsup?" Kanika said, confused and feeling silly for putting herself out there.

"Yo, chill wit' all that, Kanika," he said angrily. "I don't play games. And in my eyes, you will always be like my lil sista'," he said. He laughed uncomfortably. "Besides, Tony said your mama ain't having it."

Kanika's suspicion was proven. Though her mother was encouraging her to holla at Tyrell because he was a "good catch," all the while Tony was putting salt in the game. She planned to have a little talk with her mother.

Tyrell glared at Kanika, but when she stared back into his dark eyes she saw that familiar softness behind them. It spoke what his mouth wouldn't. He wanted her despite his tough-man talk, she thought. And she knew there was always next time. Her eighteenth birthday couldn't come soon enough.

Two

The following morning, Saturday, Kanika woke up to the sounds of pots and pans in the kitchen. It was 10:30 A.M., and though she, her mother, and Tony got in from the party around 5:00 A.M., she and her mama had their bimonthly hair appointment at We Aim to Weave in a few hours. It wasn't something that either of them would consider missing. They took extra pride in keeping not only their bodies but their hair tight, too.

Tony was still asleep, and like on most days, unless he had an important "meeting," he would sleep until the afternoon. Waleema didn't mind one bit, because she was a morning person and always joked that Tony would slow her down trying to get some over the kitchen counter as she cooked breakfast or washed dishes. And she also realized that it was better to have her man home than in the streets, with her not knowing if he'd return. Sometimes she wished Tony didn't ever have to leave the house.

Kanika was looking forward to the quiet morning and talking to her mother about what Tyrell had told her. After she helped her mother fix a quick breakfast of eggs, grits, and toast, they sat outside in the backyard, among the rows of purple and yellow tulips Waleema had planted. She had a green thumb at gardening and was also responsible for the lush green lawn. Kanika found her mama amusing, often calling her the Ghetto Martha Stewart. To their neighbors, their family life looked normal, and no one bothered them. They sponsored block parties for the kids, organized bus rides to Atlantic City and Mohegan Sun for the grown folks, and threw Fourth of July firework parties on their rooftop that people came from afar to see. Waleema even headed the neighborhood block association. The neighbors loved and respected them and considered Waleema and Tony "entrepreneurs." Their high-rolling drug lifestyle was an open secret.

"We got so much to do today. After the salon, I gotta stop by the club," Waleema said, pouring her and Kanika some orange juice.

"For what?" Kanika asked as they both sat under the umbrella protecting them from the hot sun.

"For my motherfuckin' money and to put my foot in somebody's ass. Somebody ain't paying their house fee," Waleema said. She sprinkled salt and pepper on her fried eggs.

Kanika smiled and shook her head. *Pity the fool*

to cross my mama, she thought. Her mama began stripping when she was seventeen, and she knew the business in and out. She was smart enough to open her own strip club business with Tony's money, too.

"I gotta ask you something about Tyrell," Kanika said as she looked over her shoulder.

"What?" her mother asked as she waved to her neighbor in the next backyard.

"Last night, he said that Tony said you would be pissed if he and I got together." Kanika waved to the neighbor as well.

"That's a damn lie. Wait till Tony's fat ass gets up," Waleema said with a grin. "He just don't want you with Tyrell. He thinks Tyrell is dangerous."

"Please. I live with you and Tony; what could be more dangerous than that!" Kanika said, putting down her glass of juice. "You two got more Gats and shotguns in here than Fort Knox."

"Nika," Waleema said, holding back her smile and bringing her fingers to her lips. "Good morning, Mr. Hammerstein." Waleema waved to another neighbor.

"Can we go inside?" Kanika asked as she grabbed her plate. Her mother followed as she went to sit in the living room.

"I guess Tony just don't like how wild Tyrell is. He is young, but I think with a good woman in his life, he'd be a good man. I really like Tyrell. I just think Tony is a little threatened by him."

"For real?" Kanika said, surprised by her mother's words.

Waleema confided in her like they were best friends. "Sometimes I feel like that. Tony is getting older and Tyrell is on the come up. And I know I ain't gonna be around forever, and I wanna make sure you are taken care of," Waleema said, grabbing Kanika's hands. "You are not a regular girl, Kanika. You are born in the life. We got mad drama with us going back to your grandfather in the sixties, running them numbers." She paused to laugh. "These other cats around here would just want you for your money. They would run for the hills if they knew your daddy clipped three men with his bare hands and till this day their bodies have not been found. You need to be with a man who can protect you, hide your dirty laundry, and die for you."

Kanika held her mother's hands tightly. "That must be why I can't get my mind off Tyrell. The way he looks at me, it's like different. If only Tony could see that, he'd know Tyrell would only do me good."

Waleema let her hands go as they went back to eating their food. She spread more butter on her toast. "Baby, you are like Tony's daughter. No man will ever be good enough for you. If you want Tyrell, you got my blessing."

Kanika was relieved and hugged her mother. But she still wished Tony could see what she saw in Tyrell.

"Shit! Where all my bacon go?" Kanika heard Tony shout from the kitchen. She and her mother laughed.

"You go upstairs and get ready for our appointment, while me and Tony talk."

"Not about Tyrell?"

"Child, you ain't telling your mama what to do, are you?" she said, cocking her head to the side.

"No," Kanika said, stealing a slice of bacon from her mama's plate. "Let me go get ready."

"Good idea, and don't come down until I call you," Waleema said as she disappeared into the kitchen.

Kanika knew that there was going to be more than bacon sizzling in the kitchen.

"What's good, ladies?" Sherisse said as she hugged Kanika and then Waleema. "Chantal and DeeDee are waiting for the both of you. So get ya asses in those chairs!"

Kanika and her mother were dressed in identical Iceberg Jeans, Gucci sandals, and Dolce & Gabbana tees. They walked past a row of women who were already waiting, but everyone knew not to trip. If it meant the rest of them had to wait another half hour for a stylist, they'd just have to wait.

"Peaches and I already got our outfits," Chantal, Peaches' mother, said as she undid the tracks in Kanika's hair. "Oooh, girl, I cannot wait for your party next week!"

"Thank you, Ms. Adams," Kanika said. Chantal was almost forty-five years old and Kanika didn't see why she would be so interested in going to an eighteen-year-old's birthday party. But Chantal had been around at every party Kanika had since she and Peaches started their relationship back in grade school.

"Girl, don't thank me; thank your mama," Chantal said, flashing a wide gold-capped grin.

Kanika's mother looked at her and winked. "My baby thanks me all the time with her good grades. Did she tell y'all she got accepted to Hampton *and* NYU," her mother stated more than she asked.

"No, you didn't!" DeeDee squealed as she and Chantal congratulated Kanika.

Chantal said, "I wish Peaches was that smart. All she cares about is being under some man who will let her shop until her nose bleeds."

"She ain't like that, Ms. Adams," Kanika said, sticking up for her friend.

"She wanna be like you too much. I just wish she had your brains."

Then Dee said, "Girl, what you need a degree for? Your mama's man got enough money—"

Waleema frowned. "Excuse me, Dee? I didn't hear dat." She stared DeeDee down in the mirror as Chantal and Kanika stayed quiet.

DeeDee rolled her eyes. Kanika sat back, knowing her mother was about to go off.

"Bitch, let me tell you. The next time you talk about how much money my man got, you gonna be fryin' fish in the morning," Kanika's mother said, pointing in the mirror, her eyes shooting daggers at

DeeDee. "What *we* have is none of your goddamn business."

DeeDee lowered her eyes and apologized. Everyone maintained their silence. *DeeDee should have known better,* Kanika thought. It was common knowledge that no one discussed her man's street business with anyone else but her man. And if another woman even suggested something, that was disrespectful. It put the girlfriend in an awkward situation where many friendships had been lost. Rumors and envy spread on the street faster than a good fight. DeeDee was alone, broke, and had four children from her drug-dealing former man, Reika, and two other men. Kanika's mother was no fool; she knew what was up. Tony Black was even bigger than Reika and pulling twice as many millions, at a time when the drug game was being sucked dry by the Feds. Kanika thought DeeDee was a classic case of sister hating behind a smile.

On their way home about three hours later, Kanika's mother conducted business on her cell phone. There was still an issue, as she talked with Felix, the manager of her club, about which girl wasn't paying her house fee.

"You know, you try to be friendly with some them bitches, because I was just where they are now. Then they try to shit on you," Waleema said as she pressed the phone tightly to her ear. "I want all my motherfuckin' money today. Things have changed from the days when I was stripping. We was businesswomen; you would get your ass beat if you didn't pay up. I may have to start smacking up bitches," she said, speeding down Atlantic Avenue. "Or *your* ass is gonna catch it!"

Kanika didn't know what was going on, but she knew that with each breath her mother's voice was getting louder and louder.

Waleema pulled her SUV into the parking lot of the Kitty Lounge, the club she had owned and operated for six years, since she was twenty-nine. Her mother slipped on her black shades and flung her Gucci bag over her shoulder. But when Kanika saw her mama's lively pace, she knew she was about to pull out a can of whip ass on someone. Her mother urged her to stay behind in case things got ugly.

It was around 2:00 P.M., and the club was holding their afternoon show. Kanika slipped in through the back door and walked up the squeaky, steep steps. It was only a few times that she had been inside, but the images were embedded in her brain. Buck naked women freely walked back and forth applying makeup, gossiping, or smoking in the dressing rooms. Their bodies were different hues of brown, shiny, toned, and well maintained. Some were light skinned or dark, short-haired, long-haired, shaved, unshaved, thick in the waist, hauling huge asses that would put hers to shame, tall like models, with smaller asses and breasts, and the rest were in between. There was something for every man's fantasy. It was exactly what her mother was good at, knowing what men wanted and needed.

From the top of the steps, Kanika heard the loud bass of a popular booty song being pumped through the walls. She looked onto the stage from the side and saw a naked brown-skinned woman wearing only a glittery bra slide down the silver pole. Festive twinkling lights hung from every corner and from the bar's perimeter. Kanika wondered how her own mother had looked, because this was the exact same club she had worked at in her stripping days, though now she owned it and the adjacent parking lot. Kanika wasn't ashamed that her mama had started out as a stripper. Shit, Waleema did what she had to do and she had been one of the best in the business. There was a reason that Waleema was the "top bitch" behind the "head nigga in charge." She had also passed on some good beauty techniques to Kanika along the way.

Kanika heard loud voices coming from another room, which sounded like yells. She put her ear to the door, which was closed.

"Listen, bitch, I don't care if I have to search your motherfuckin' ass, I will get my money today—right now!" Waleema demanded.

There was a muffled whisper.

"What, bitch?" Waleema said. "And you think that makes you special? Just because I gave you a little taste? You lucky I don't make you get on your knees right now!"

"Waleema, please, just listen to me. I had to use the money to—"

A glass shattered against the wall. Kanika wondered if her mother was in any danger and opened the door slightly. Face-to-face were Waleema and a young light-skinned woman pointing at each other. Kanika's mother kept her finger in the woman's face and threatened her.

"I see you wanna play games," Waleema said, turning around. She started going through all the dresser drawers in the room. She pulled out stacks of singles, then turned back around and backhand-slapped the girl so hard, Kanika stopped breathing. She had never seen her mother so angry, and it made her angry. She wanted to go in that room and step on that woman's face for getting her mother all riled up. *She got what she deserved*, Kanika thought.

Waleema continued to walk around the room, opening and closing drawers. The young woman got up and begged Kanika's mother for forgiveness.

"Waleema, can you just look at me? I am so sorry, please," she said, on her knees, her hands on Waleema's thighs.

Waleema kicked her foot out, knocking the girl back on the floor. The girl crawled to the closet and handed over all the money she owed. She cried, holding her reddened face. Kanika's mother didn't even look up until she'd counted every bill.

"I saved your skinny ass when you was giving niggas head for twenty dollars on Hunts Point. And now you wanna steal from me?" Waleema said as she stuffed the bills inside her bra. "Get the fuck outta my place. Trick-ass bitch."

Kanika took that as her cue to get her behind back in the car. She inched away from the door and quickly walked past the women's dressing room and heard several women laughing. It seemed that they all knew what was going on. But Kanika froze when one woman spoke.

"I guess another one bites the dust. Cherry was so stupid. Just because she ate Waleema's pussy a few times, she think she can get away with some crazy shit like not payin' her house fee. Dumb bitch. . . ."

Then another girl spoke. "I think after she did that threesome with Waleema and Tony she probably thought she was part of the fuckin' family. So to speak. . . ." There were some more laughs.

"We all had to dip our spoon in Waleema's puddin' to get down. It's part of the damn interview. And no other booty bar pays like she does." There was another roar of laughter.

Kanika raced down the steps so fast she almost tripped. She ran past an older man who was walking up the steps, and bolted through the door. She locked herself inside the car, her mind racing. She never knew that her mother got down like that. Though she guessed she shouldn't have been surprised. Waleema regulated everything with her sex, from her business to her man. Tony was a lion in the streets but a lamb in the sheets. Kanika had always sensed that her mother had a little bit of freak in her. She didn't know about the threesome with Tony, but on more than one occasion she had heard Waleema and Tony tearing it up, sounding like two animals in heat. But damn. . . .

In a few minutes Waleema got in the car and put it in gear. There were enough singles in her bag that they were spilling out.

"Everything OK, baby?" Kanika's mother asked, hitting the gas.

"Yes. I just can't wait for my party." Kanika didn't want to get all in her mama's business, but she was chewing on every little detail.

Three

Kanika had it all planned for her eighteenth birthday party. It was a sunny July afternoon and she knew that tonight more than champagne was getting popped. In her thoughts all day was fine-ass Tyrell. She wasn't worried about him bringing any chicks with him this time, because he would never play her like that at her own birthday party. She spent almost three hours at Golden Silk Spa, a high-end salon in the city, getting her body scrubbed, wrapped, and massaged. She wanted her skin to taste like sugar on Tyrell's tongue. She was not sure how she was going to do it, but she had to spice things up. Her mama seemed to have men and women at her whim, but Kanika just wanted one man. And by the end of tonight she planned to become a woman in his eyes.

The Diamond Princess Ballroom in Bed-Stuy was a popular venue for neighborhood wedding receptions, but it was also known to be the place where big spenders would throw their private ghetto-fabulous events. Waleema made sure Kanika's party was equipped with the number-one hip-hop DJ in all of New York, who was also one of Tony's main customers and oldest friends. Not to mention dozens of cases of Cristal, Dom P., and Henny, imported snow crab legs and jumbo shrimp, and plenty of barbecue short ribs, because those were some of Kanika's favorites.

But this day was important not only to Kanika but to her mother, too. By Kanika's age, Waleema was stripping and had been living with Shon, Kanika's daddy, then one of Harlem's best-paid drug king-pins, now holding his reign in Virginia. She no longer kept in contact with Shon, but with his help she had managed to build an impressive trust fund for Kanika so that if she never wanted to work she didn't have to. Waleema made sure Kanika had a solid education not only in the streets but also of the world. The only thing she wanted Kanika to shake for a dollar was her college degree. And maybe one day a diamond ring from Tyrell, the only man Waleema believed was worthy.

Tony and Tyrell and the rest of his capos had their own table off to the side of the magnificently sized ballroom. There was some concern that Cee-Lo's people weren't going away as easy as they thought. Things had been real quiet on the streets for about a month, until one of Tony's spots got shot up the night before. Also, Kevin Lyons, one of the hit men of the group, was shot in the altercation. The police were breathing down Tony's back and everyone else's since that had gone down. This frustrated Tyrell because out of everyone, he alone knew that clipping Cee-Lo was an all-around bad idea.

"I'm telling y'all, all we gotta do is cap that nigga Blake. That's that nigga who got away. His ass supposed to be six feet with Cee-Lo," Kevin said, his tattooed arm resting on his crutch. Kevin was one of those niggas who would do anything. That's why Tyrell kept him on his team to do the dirty work. His being 300 pounds helped, too.

"Fuck that. That's the shit that got us where we is now!" Tyrell said, shooting a glance at Tony. "Them motherfuckas is like us. Yeah, Cee-Lo only had like five boys in his whole crew, but them niggas got heart. I went to school with them niggas. Just because it looked like they took their asses back down south because of the po-po after Cee-Lo got clipped don't mean shit. Their asses is like roaches: no matter what you do, they gonna keep coming back."

Tony picked at his teeth with a toothpick as he snarled at Tyrell, "Why can't you understand what I'm trying to do here? If I didn't drop that motherfucka, he woulda clipped *my* ass. You think I had that motherfucka up at night thinking how we can be friends?"

"I don't think that's what Tyrell is saying, man," Kevin said, looking agitated. "What happened the other night is gonna get closer to home. We all hot."

Tyrell interrupted, facing Tony. "With all due respect, man, I ain't talking about being friends. I'm talking about business partners. Either niggas keep clipping motherfuckas or we all sit down and come to some negotiations. I'd rather sit down and multiply our motherfuckin' shit."

"Sit down? So niggas can take over mines?" Tony said, patting his chest like he was King Kong.

"See, that's a problem there," Tyrell said, shaking his head. "You supposed to give niggas a chance to break bread with you. I may be young, but I'm old-school. I ain't no fuckin' animal going around clipping niggas and ain't getting shit from it, yo. I clipped one nigga 'cause I was protecting mine. The other two was 'cause I was getting mine."

"So what you saying?" Tony asked, as everyone leaned forward to listen.

"We sit down with Cee-Lo's connects and see how we can bring our shit together. We got their shit now, but nobody know their hustle like the nigga who's hustling. What we got we can't handle. All that Bronx shit is their territory. We don't got no connects up there. We can give them twenty percent, if they agree to push their work in their area, and they get to keep their motherfuckin' lives." He poured himself another glass of Henny, his large forearm showing a distinctive tattoo of a woman's face. "I know them niggas; they're workers. All they wanna do is eat. And if they ain't with no deal, I'm catching bodies."

"Word . . . that's the truth right there," said a few voices, and everyone nodded.

"Well, let me sleep on it," Tony said, his brow furrowed in thought. "You sure you ain't really Italian, motherfucka?" Everyone cracked up because they knew Tony wasn't much of a negotiator and that's why he had Tyrell. And though he didn't show it, Tyrell was who was keeping Tony's hustle running like a well-oiled machine.

Kanika sat at a table with family and friends, watching Tyrell from afar. He was the only one dressed in a sharp, crisp tan linen suit and wingtipped alligator shoes. His clothing draped his tall, sturdy build like a king. He looked so in command, she thought, with his exaggerated hand gestures and intense eye contact with everyone as they listened. When he laughed, he looked even more handsome. Their eyes greeted each other for a brief moment and he winked at her. Before she could walk over, a few other guys gathered around the table. One of them was RaKing, one of the hottest music producers out now, who used to run with Tony back in the day. She thought RaKing was a cutie, and he reminded her of Roy Jones Jr.

A skintight champagne-colored Versace-inspired dress, handpicked by her mother, accentuated the richness of Kanika's smooth, dark sin. She was looking especially good tonight; her hair was loose on her shoulders, in a wavy style that complemented her

Asian-looking eyes and voluptuous lips. As soon as Tony left the table, she made her approach. Tyrell stood up and RaKing took notice.

"You sure you just eighteen?" RaKing asked, checking her out from the back.

"Yes," Kanika said, but she looked at Tyrell.

"Damn!" RaKing shouted, biting his knuckles. "You sure is one hot young thing."

"Aight, man, chill," Tyrell said, stepping around the table to Kanika.

Yes, yes, she thought. *Now tell him I'm all yours.*

"She's like my lil sis. Fall back, man." RaKing and Tyrell laughed, but Kanika didn't. The other guys were already dispersing out to the bar.

"Happy birthday," Tyrell said, as he hugged Kanika in a tight embrace. He kissed her forehead.

Kanika was pissed. Was that it? No mouth action? No sexy whisper in her ear? Even RaKing acknowledged how fine she was.

"Thank you," Kanika said. She took Tyrell's hands. "Can we talk for a minute?"

"Um, let me finish up here, and I'll catch up with you. Don't worry; I got your gift right here," he said, waving what looked like a money holder. Every year Tyrell gave her money.

"I don't want *that* as a gift," she said into Tyrell's ear.

Tyrell smiled uncomfortably. "I'll holla at you later."

"Yeah, shorty. *We* gonna dance later, right?"

RaKing said, taking Kanika's hands. He kissed them. "I'ma be waiting right here."

Kanika wanted to snatch her hands away, but she let him kiss them.

Tyrell hissed at RaKing, "Yo, man, I said chill."

"You promise?" Kanika said in her sexiest voice.

"I need to talk to you for a minute, young lady," Tony said, behind her. She walked away, leaving RaKing with a gaping mouth and Tyrell with a screwed-up face. She followed Tony to a private room, where all her gifts were being kept.

He closed the door to keep out the noise. "Don't be getting too caught up in that nigga."

"Who? RaKing?" Kanika asked, knowing damn well what the deal was. She dug her hands into a bowl of barbecue chips.

"Tyrell. I don't want to see you get hurt in all this. Know what I mean?" Tony and Kanika sat down on the long beige leather sofa. "He's into a lot of complicated shit. Plus, he got mad women."

"Whatever, Tony. How you gonna put salt in his game like that?" Kanika said, shaking her head. Then she paused. "Women like who?"

"Like Cee-Lo's ex-chick. But I ain't about to be putting the man's business out there. Just watch yourself or I'm gonna have to get involved."

If she wanted to get with Tyrell, she thought, she was going to have to lie to Tony. "Please, I mean, Tyrell is good-looking and all, but I'm not into him like that. It's like a crush; it's not serious."

"Women. Y'all always gotta learn the hard way," Tony huffed. "Life will make you grow up soon enough." Tony finally smiled. His black pupils dilated under the shimmery chandelier lights. "I wanna give this to you now," he said, pulling out a tiny blue box.

Kanika put her hand over her mouth and held the box in her palm. She opened it and saw an exquisite necklace, with a three-inch K initial decked out in pink diamonds and platinum. Water welled up in her eyes as she held the precious jewel in her hand. Tony turned her around and fastened the chain around her neck.

"Tony, this is beautiful!" she cried. "I don't know what to say."

"Just make sure you thank your mama, too. She helped me pick it out," he said, with a smug smile. "Read the back."

Kanika turned the pendant around. She read: *Death before Dishonor*.

Tony Black stared at her, intently nodding his head.

"Yes," Kanika said in a weak tone, and hugged him. "I know what's up. Thank you, again."

"We love you, girl, and we proud of you," Tony Black said, and kissed her forehead.

Kanika closed her eyes and another tear dropped. She looked into his eyes and saw something she never saw before. *Fear.* With all that was going on in the last few weeks, Tony wasn't so sure how it would all end.

Then the door knocked and opened. "Why you

got my baby girl all cryin' on her special day?" Kanika's mother said, sitting on Tony's lap. "Nika, you like the chain?"

Kanika's eyes brightened up. "These are tears of joy, Mama. I love this. Just wait till my girls see this."

Her mama and Tony stared at her and then each other. Kanika decided to walk out and give them their privacy. They were notorious for getting it on whenever, however.

Kanika sailed through the ballroom, being stopped every five seconds by another face. She had to admit to herself that she did look on top of her game tonight. And by looking around she could understand why people like Chantal were excited about her party. Anyone who was anyone was there, from paid street hustlers and OGs to music industry cats. Some of Kanika's school friends were there, too, but she liked to keep her circle small. Many of the girls at school either hated or loved her, and she liked it that way.

"Girl, you are lookin' fierce tonight. Dat chain is bad! I would die to have one of those."

Kanika giggled, holding up the pendant like the rappers did in the videos.

"Do you know that RaKing has been looking for you?" Peaches said, wearing a black and gold prom-like dress Kanika thought was a bit too small for her large frame.

"Where is he? I'm gonna show Tyrell how to man up when it comes to me," she said.

Kanika marched off and spotted RaKing right away. He was talking to Tyrell.

Perfect, she thought.

"Hello, fellas," Kanika cooed.

RaKing quickly put down his drink and took her hand. "Finally, I get my dance?"

Kanika followed him to the dance floor, where reggae music had everybody getting low and grinding slow.

RaKing wrapped his arms around her body and pressed her close. She laid her head on his shoulder and smiled at Tyrell. He turned his back. The reggae beat picked up a tempo or two as Kanika and RaKing bumped their bodies against each other. Kanika was really feeling RaKing's moves and it showed. She rolled her hips into his middle, letting him feel her ass and thighs. The lights were dim, with tints of red, and RaKing's hardness pressed on her lower back. He held on to her waist as they both bent back into the groove of the song. Everyone else on the dance floor was getting just as loose. RaKing got down low and his face met Kanika's thighs, her stomach, and rose up to her breasts. The bass thumped louder and their bodies danced harder. Kanika's back dampened with sweat as Raking massaged it up and down.

Then RaKing turned around. Tyrell was tapping him on the shoulder.

"Yo, nigga, what you want?" RaKing asked, his hands locked around Kanika's tiny waist.

"You two need to chill. You disrespecting her, yo," Tyrell said, towering over RaKing.

"Nigga, please," RaKing spewed as he went back to dancing. But Kanika stiffened. She didn't want any problems, and from the looks of Tyrell there were about to be some.

"Uhm, RaKing, I have to go the bathroom," Kanika said, as Tyrell stood by.

"Come on, let's finish this song, boo," RaKing said, pulling Kanika into him.

Tyrell grabbed RaKing by his neck and dragged him off the dance floor like he was a rag doll. Several other men followed him. Kanika didn't know what happened next, but all she heard was a lot of yells and what sounded like a beatdown going on outside. In about ten minutes, Tyrell was back looking annoyed.

"Nika, what the fuck is your problem?" Waleema said, taking Kanika by her elbow. They both proceeded to an empty room, where Waleema locked the door.

"Is you trying to get niggas toasted? I spent way too much time and money on this party," she said, drilling her words into Kanika's face.

"I'm sorry," Kanika said, looking away. "I just wanted Tyrell to notice me. Now he's probably mad at me."

"Honey, sit down." Waleema patted Kanika's shoulders. "Tyrell really likes you. But he's gonna keep treating you like some lil sister as long as you keep acting like one. Dancing all hard on that Ra-King nigga brings out all of Tyrell's jealous-man instincts. He's gonna start seeing you as a liability, not an asset. To be with a man like Tyrell you gotta show and prove you can hold your own." Waleema handed Kanika some tissue from her purse. "He'll make his move; just give him a chance."

"But what about Tony? Earlier he told me I shouldn't be fuckin' with Tyrell."

"I told you I'd handle Tony. He won't be telling you that shit no more. Just go back out there and have a good time."

"That's exactly what I'm gonna do," Kanika said, blowing into a tissue.

"Just keep looking good doing it," Waleema said as they both grinned. "Now get up off me and go do your thing. This is *your* night."

As soon as they stepped out of the room, a five-tier white-frosted Italian hand-crafted cake was wheeled out. Everyone, including Tyrell, gathered around the perimeter of the dance floor and sang "Happy Birthday" to Kanika. She felt so embarrassed, she covered her face with her hands. The spotlight was on her and she knew she had to come up with a wish soon.

"Make a wish and blow out the candle, child," she heard a woman's voice somewhere in the crowd say. Since Kanika couldn't blow out the huge mass of candles on the cake, a small slice was bought to her with a sole candle. When everyone silenced themselves, she closed her eyes, made a wish, and blew it out. She wished for Tyrell's heart and her family's safety.

Kanika was immersed in attention and good wishes from her family and guests. Again she caught Tyrell staring at her.

"Sorry if I made a scene earlier, but I was a little jealous. Just a little," he said, handing her his envelope.

She opened it. Five hundred-dollar bills were inside.

"You can use it for school," he said, stroking her face.

"Thank you." Kanika handed the envelope back to him. "But I got enough money for school."

"Hold on," he said, as Kanika began to walk away. "I still want you to have it."

"Tyrell, the only thing I need from you, you can't give me."

"It ain't as easy as it looks. I gotta respect other people's wishes," he said, leaving the envelope on the table.

Kanika thought he was referring to Tony.

Then the beat blasted again from the overhead speakers and the party was back on. Cake slices and Cristal champagne were delivered to everyone's table.

At the end of the evening, the crowd began to thin out. Kanika was tired, and her feet hurt. Tonight had been one of the best nights of her life. She was finally eighteen. But she could still think of one more thing to make it better.

"Mommy, I'm tired. Can I leave with you and Tony?" Kanika asked. "Peaches is going out to another party and I just ain't in the mood for anything else."

"Sure, baby, but Tony and I gotta stop by the club. I'll have Tyrell drop you home." Her mother smiled and downed her last glass of champagne.

"Tyrell?" Kanika asked, surprised, but she knew.

"Yes, and he's about to leave. Go tell him your mama said for him to drop you home." Kanika's mother peered into her face. *"And don't wait up for us."*

Four

Tyrell dropped Kanika home in his sleek black Acura Legend after her birthday party. They didn't talk much because he spent most of his time on the cell phone fielding calls from his "street team." But inside his air-conditioned, comfortable ride, fully equipped with spinning shiny rims, Kanika didn't want to leave. She thought about how much she could get used to this.

Kanika opened the door to Tony's four-family mansion-style home in Bed-Stuy. It had twelve rooms and nine bathrooms, with a furnished basement she and her mother were never allowed to enter.

"Do you wanna come in?" Kanika asked Tyrell, who was waiting by the door. She could tell he really wanted to.

"I don't mind if I do," he said, walking in. Kanika could tell something was going on. That Tyrell had something on his mind, not about her but about business. Her mother had always told her to never ask a man about his business, but she was too nosy for her own good.

"So what was you and Tony talkin' about all night?"

"Nothin' much. I just notice any time you and I are together he shows up," Tyrell spit.

Kanika felt alarmed at his angry tone but turned on, too. "I know, but he just really cares about me. Is that so bad?"

Tyrell only looked at her as if he did not understand.

"So what is up with that light-skinned chick I be seeing you with. Cee-Lo's ex?" she asked.

"She ain't my girl." Tyrell smirked. "She's the round-the-way chick. Everybody hit that. She was Cee-Lo's jump-off."

"So why she be hanging with you?"

"Man, listen. That one time she popped up on me. She like what a brother rollin' with. I just ain't feeling her like that."

"So it's a sex thing?"

He didn't know how to answer that and paused. "It's a sex thing. But I haven't hit that in a minute."

Kanika was relieved to know that wasn't his girl. She could care less if he had sex with her. That was his business. Once she got Tyrell in her bed, there would be no need for him to go elsewhere.

They flipped channels and watched TV like they

had done for years. But tonight was different. There was a comfort zone that was opening up between her and Tyrell. Their shoulders were touching, and as they watched BET videos she even put one of her legs across his lap.

"Tyrell," Kanika began, a bit nervous as to what was about to happen. "You know I like you."

Tyrell turned to her and got in her face, close enough for her to feel his breath. He gazed at her like he usually did, and the softness behind his eyes appeared. He didn't have the stress on his face he had had all night.

He kissed her lips. Kanika's lips trembled, because he had never made an advance before. Then he pulled away.

Kanika wasn't going to miss her chance again. She grabbed his neck and pulled his mouth down toward her. They kissed hard and long like they had at her mother and Tony's party. Tyrell hungrily searched her mouth with his. He picked her up and sat her on his lap. They kissed and petted each other for what seemed like hours. He kissed the top part of her breasts squeezing out of her dress. She bent her neck back and pressed her pussy into his hardened dick.

"Is it your first time?" Tyrell asked, holding her shoulders.

Kanika wanted to lie and say it wasn't. She looked away and felt that he really would think she was a little girl. "It is."

Tyrell's demeanor changed and he caressed her more slowly, gently. His eyes remained soft and gentle, which completely relaxed Kanika as she slipped out of her clothes. He helped her. She stood before him, naked, her hips rounded and her breasts high and nipples pointed upward.

"Let's go in the bedroom," Tyrell instructed as he took her hand. He shut the door behind them and he began to undress himself with precision and ease. Kanika flicked the lights off and slid under the covers. She was self-conscious about being naked in front of a man. She pulled the covers up to her chin. Tyrell slipped his hard, warm body on top of hers and ran his strong hands over her fleshy ass. Every part of her was alive as she spread her legs underneath him. He slipped farther down and kissed her breasts, stomach, thighs. He licked her pussy with light strokes. Kanika's toes curled so hard they hurt. He licked her more feverishly, taking her whole pussy into his mouth. She could tell he was feasting on being the first man to ever get that close to her. It was like uncharted land, and Kanika wanted him to make her body his home. When Tyrell rose back up, his face glistened with her juices, because by now she was ready. He slipped on a condom and entered her, inch by inch, until he was in.

Kanika cried out. It was a cry that made her insides gel. It shook her to her core. But Tyrell didn't waver. He kept stroking steady and slow, until her muscles were completely relaxed. She locked her legs around him, like she didn't want to let go. He rocked her body hard, and then slow, in the same position until every wall inside her opened up to him. He knew exactly what he was doing, and Kanika wondered how much practice he had. But what she was feeling far outweighed any doubt in her mind that he was the One.

After they finished, they lay beside each other in the dark. There was no music, no light, just the sound of their breathing. She laid her head across Tyrell's chest as he stroked her hair. It was 3:00 A.M., and they had been alone for two hours. She wondered if her mom was home. Her room was a floor above. But Kanika didn't hear anything.

"What's wrong?" Tyrell asked in his deep, smooth voice.

"Ain't nothin' wrong," Kanika's voice shook. She rubbed his six-pack.

"Don't start lying already."

"Whatchu mean?"

"I can feel your heart racing. Somethin' is on your mind," he said, and kissed her bare shoulder.

"Mommy hasn't come home yet," she said, feeling silly. She wanted to show Tyrell she was grown, and whining about her mother wasn't a place to start.

"I'm here. You ain't alone in this big-ass house. Besides, they probably still at the club."

She looked up at him. He made her feel safe. She kissed his thick, juicy lips. He was so dark that only the white of his eyes and teeth showed in the dark.

She straddled him as he stroked her flat stomach and caressed her breasts. He sat up and sucked on her nipple like a baby. Then bit it, making her jump. He bit it again. She jumped at the unusual pain of pleasure.

"Do it again," she said, holding her nipple to his mouth. He laughed and wrapped her pointy nipple in his hot, soft tongue.

"I'm gonna show you how I like it," he said, kissing her neck and sucking on her soft flesh. He was rougher this time as he flipped her on her stomach.

"I've always loved this ass," he said, kneading it like dough with his hands. "You definitely got it from your mama."

Kanika giggled. She lay still as she gave up her ass for Tyrell's worship. She had known men liked it, but not how much, until now. Tyrell gently bit around her plump ass cheeks, then smacked them.

"Oooh," Kanika moaned at the feeling it brought to her pussy.

"You like that?" he asked, doing it again.

Kanika arched her back some more to raise her ass even higher.

Tyrell kept his tongue loose and painted wide circles around the flesh of Kanika's ass. She couldn't help thinking of an argument she had heard when Tyrell said to Tony, *"I don't kiss nobody's ass!"* The *rules change ever so quickly,* she thought.

Kanika grimaced at the funny feeling, but Tyrell seemed lost inside her ass cheeks. Not holding back one bit, she moaned louder at the feeling and brought her hand down to her pussy to play with herself. And before she knew it, she was on her knees and Tyrell was stroking her pussy from behind. It felt better than the first time, she thought. Tyrell pulled her hips back, holding them tight, letting go only to smack her ass. And then she heard him let out a lion's roar, and he collapsed next to her.

She crawled over next to him as he lay breathless on his back. Kanika thought this was a good time to examine his dick. She flipped the night-light on and saw why it had hurt so bad the first time. She couldn't believe she had gotten that massive anaconda-sized dick inside her body. Her exceptional math skills counted that he was at least eleven and a half inches long, uncircumcised. As she surveyed his shrinking dick, she touched it and rubbed it on her face. It felt hot and smooth and looked like black satin. Her mouth watered as she thought about chocolate and how some would be good in her mouth right now. Tyrell kept his eyes shut and rubbed Kanika's back. She gripped his dick in her hand and kissed her way down its length.

Tyrell moaned and gripped her hair in his hand. She hadn't heard him moan like that earlier. She put two more kisses on the other side of his dick, this time closer to the head. He moaned some more. She made her mouth real wet and slid what was now about six inches firm into her mouth. She sucked his swollen head until it grew to its proud length, but it was just too much to handle for her first time. But whatever she was doing, it was working, because Tyrell was like putty in her hands. He was calling her "baby" and saying "shit" so many times, she had to wonder if there was someone else in the room.

By 5:00 A.M. Tyrell lay awake while Kanika slept by his side. He thought about the first time he'd met Kanika, years ago, when she was a little girl. Their age difference gave him a compelling need to protect her. That need slowly grew into a desire to love her. He'd loved her from the start, he realized. It had nothing to do with her stepping to him like a woman like she had in the cigar room, though it had let him know she was feeling him, too. And if there was anything he could thank Tony for, it was introducing him to Kanika. But that was it. Any respect and love he had had for him was being challenged now. Tony was fucking up, and his fuck-up could mess up any future he could have with Kanika. And it was Kanika he wanted to live for.

Five

Kanika dreamed that someone was calling her name. "Nika, Nika . . ." She opened her eyes and saw Tyrell hovering over her, looking chiseled.

"Yo, I gotta go. We'll talk, later," he said, getting out of bed and getting dressed.

Kanika hopped out of the bed, ran to the window, and breathed a sigh of relief. It was 8:00 A.M., and her mom and Tony's car was outside. But Kanika wasn't too concerned about Tyrell running into Tony, who would be asleep for a few more hours. She walked over to Tyrell and ran her hands over his hair-speckled chest.

"Why can't you stay a lil longer? Tony don't wake up until noon at least." She sat on the bed and pulled Tyrell down, hoping to entice him, but he moved her hand away.

"I got some business to take care of," he said,

slipping his platinum chain over his neck. "I'll holla at you later. Aight?"

"Well, what kind of business you gotta do so early? On a Sunday?"

Tyrell exhaled and said, "Look, first off, you can't be asking me about my business. But if you must know, I gotta go to church."

Kanika stared at him in disbelief. "Church? You go to church?" she asked, realizing that Tyrell got more interesting the more she learned about him.

Tyrell shot up from the bed, checked his pockets, and grabbed his keys. He bent down and planted a fat, juicy kiss on Kanika's still-astonished open mouth. He closed the bedroom door and let himself out.

Kanika went to the window and saw him hop in his car and drive off with a quickness. She prayed that Tyrell wasn't already trying to play her, because he would definitely be the one to get played. *No nigga I know go to church.* But then again, church was probably the only place where he felt safe. And if there was anyone she thought needed church, it was a man like Tyrell.

By midafternoon and after a long well-deserved nap, Kanika decided to chill in the living room. Waleema and Tony were already on the couch giggling like two teenagers. He had Waleema's feet in his hands, giving them a tender massage.

"Am I interrupting something?" Kanika grinned. "I can come back."

"Nika, if a man massages your feet, he doesn't need to do anything else to prove his love," Tony said, smiling at Waleema. "Ain't that right, baby?"

"If he sucks your toes, then he really loves you." Waleema stuck her foot in Tony's face. And he playfully sucked each of her bare toes.

"Ugh, come on, y'all. I just woke up," Kanika said, covering her eyes. "You two need to leave some things to the imagination."

Tony laughed and got up. "I'ma leave you two alone. But last I heard, if a woman really loves a man she brings him his breakfast in bed." And he ascended the stairs.

"You see how these men are," Waleema said, getting up and heading to the kitchen. "Wanna help me make his plate?"

Kanika walked into the kitchen trying to look normal in spite of having spent the night with Tyrell.

Her mother stared at her up and down and all around. Waleema sniffed around her neck. Stepped back and broke out into a loud laugh. "No, you didn't," she said, taking out an empty glass from the cupboard.

"Didn't what?" Kanika said, with her mouth half-full, holding an empty yellow mug for Tony's milk. That was all he drank in the mornings.

"You and Tyrell?" her mother asked, tapping her fingers against the chrome sink.

Waleema wasn't going to flip or get angry if she told her the truth, Kanika thought. But she still felt funny about being so open with her. She was eighteen now and her business was her business only. "What about us?"

"Hmph," her mother said, reaching for a yellow serving tray. She sauntered around the yellow kitchen in a black lace nightie and heels and pulled out a wooden chair at the kitchen table. "Sit down, please."

Kanika pulled out a chair and sat down also. She was worried that she could be in trouble.

"Did you fuck Tyrell?"

"Yes," Kanika said, after a brief hesitation. "But Mommy, he was my first."

"Did you use protection?"

"Yes," Kanika said, but they hadn't the second time.

Kanika's mother's lips formed a smile. "He a good brother. And he come from a good family. Despite the fact that, well, you know he makes his living in clandestine ways."

"I guess," Kanika said.

"Just want to make sure you keep your head out of the clouds. The streets come first with men like Tyrell," she said. "But I knew his ass would be outta here to get to church this morning. You shoulda went wit' him."

The idea that Waleema had planned the whole thing came to Kanika's mind. Waleema had known that she and Tyrell would be home alone for hours. But she just listened.

"Now, Kanika, Tyrell is a serious kind of brother.

He don't play. And if you gonna go around here be-ing his woman that means a lot of responsibility is gonna fall on you. Your main thing is to keep him satisfied, focused, and motivated. If you got any complaints, you come to me. Ya hear?"

"Well, what about what *I* want?" Kanika didn't see herself being a doormat. She wanted time, quality time, with any man. And she wanted to be respected. She had to know where her man was at all times.

"There is no what *you* want. It's about what *we* need. And if you play your cards right, you will have Tyrell eating out of your hands. The more money Tony stacks, the more Tyrell stacks."

Kanika nodded. That didn't exactly make her feel any better. *What good is it having a man with money if you can't spend any time with him?* she thought. She had always imagined being Tyrell's woman would mean getting showered with gifts and atten-tion and, of course, respect.

"Good, now, a few more things," Waleema said, lighting a cigarette. She opened the large kitchen windows to let the smoke go out.

"There's more?" Kanika asked, already embar-rassed that she needed this type of initiation. She felt she knew what she wanted already.

Kanika's mother puffed a round, white smoke ring into the air. "How was the sex?"

"Mommy, please. That is too personal," Kanika said, shaking her head. She covered her face with her hair. "I forgot."

"Child, with that glow on your face, the only thing you forgot was keeping your panties on!" She laughed as she got up to start making up Tony's breakfast plate of bacon and warm blueberry pancakes.

Kanika shook her head again. This was her mother, and she was always outspoken. And Kanika liked that because there were never any guessing games.

"I can tell by how you walked this morning that you feeling mighty good. Am I right?" Waleema blew out some more smoke and began to water her plants.

"Maybe."

"Look, I'm not gonna embarrass you anymore, but there are some things you need to know, since it was your first time. Never deny him. In the middle of the night, and you tired with a headache, never say no. Keep your body smelling good and clean at all times. Try anything he wants to try. Your body is not only yours now, but his. Let him know that. When you get your period, give him head. And don't be afraid to suck his dick. A good dick suck will turn a man into a thumb-sucking baby."

That caught Kanika's attention. "It will?" None of her friends had any of this inside info from a parent, and she felt lucky. She didn't have to turn to TV or books for hers.

"Yes, honey," Waleema said, adjusting some purple lilies by the kitchen windowsill. She took one and placed it in a delicate vase on Tony's tray. "It takes practice. Just remember these three things:

relax, felate, release. And release simply means to
breathe through your nose. You never want to let the
dick out of ya mouth until you done. There's more,
but I'll dish it out over time. Understand?"

"Yes, ma'am." Kanika smiled sheepishly. She
thought she had learned enough.

For the next three weeks, Kanika was attached to
Tyrell's hip like his .45. They went everywhere from
Red Lobster, to the movies, to fine seafood restau-
rants on City Island. And they were having sex
everywhere, too. One time, Tyrell snuck into the
women's bathroom at Red Lobster and gave her oral
sex after eating a platter of oysters. It was the first
time she came, and Tyrell licked up every drop of
her juices. They were definitely clicking on a whole
new level, and Kanika just didn't see Tyrell treating
her like a doormat like guys like him often did. He
held the doors for her; he never raised his voice,
even when she got on his nerves. And he always
touched her with a soft delicateness that made her
feel like fine crystal. She couldn't think of any other
man who could ever compete with this feeling.
Though Tyrell's time was split between her and the
streets, he made their time together valuable.

And last Sunday she even got the chance to go to
church with him. She was shocked to learn that he
knew all the church songs, but she did her best to
follow along. He even knew the reverend, who personally shook his hand and the hands of a few others

before he began his sermon. She thought Tyrell was a man with a conscience who might not be living this life forever, their life. It made her believe that he was more than "da man," but he was a man, with layers to reach that she only hoped to unfold.

"Mmmm, these whipped sweet potatoes taste just like Mommy's," Kanika said, as she forked some into her mouth. She watched Tyrell ravage his third piece of fried chicken wings like they were about to fly away. He just shook his head.

They were having lunch at Ruthie's, a soul food spot in Brooklyn, where people traveled from afar for a taste of the famous smothered chicken.

"Damn, I'd marry you if you could learn to cook like this," Tyrell said, with a grin. "This mac and cheese ain't no joke."

Kanika winced. She couldn't cook a thing but frozen pizza. That was one thing her mama forgot to teach her. But Waleema did say, with the right man, Kanika should be going out to dinner anyway. And that was what it looked like she and Tyrell would be doing most of the time. He was dressed in some loose jeans, a white muscle T-shirt, and his signature platinum chain. Kanika noticed that there was a set of girls across from him checking out his stellar physique. And she didn't mind one bit.

She continued eating her smothered chicken, careful not to get anything on her white tube top and matching white Iceberg jeans and gold belt. A bit of gravy sat on her top lip, and Tyrell gingerly wiped it away with a napkin. He always made sure she was well taken care of, she thought.

"Yo, your moms musta said something to Tony, because he had a word with me the other day," Tyrell said, cleaning his fingers with a napkin.

Kanika nodded happily. Her mother always knew what to say to Tony. Kanika hoped now she and Tyrell could be more open about their relationship with Tony around.

"Motherfucka threatened me. Said that if anything happened to you he would personally clip me himself—with his hand. And you know niggas like Tony never touch shit—food [drugs] or bodies."

Kanika touched her neck. She felt like she had lost all her breath. She inhaled slowly. "What? My moms said she was gonna talk to him. He must have been joking."

"Whatever, yo. All I'm saying is I may have to talk to him again. All three of us. Just lay this shit out in the open. Your moms, too. Obviously, what she said didn't mean shit."

"I don't care what Tony says. He can't be telling me who I can see and can't see. I'll just have to give him a piece of my mind. I ain't my mother."

"Don't ever disrespect Tony. He looked out for your fam'. He and I need to handle this man-to-man." Tyrell went back to his food to signal the end of that topic.

"So, what time you wanna get together later?" she asked. She and Tyrell had been spending most of their alone time at his place, because though Tony hadn't been stressing her about Tyrell, she had to give him some kind of respect. Tyrell had a luxurious three-bedroom duplex in Clinton Hill equipped with state-of-the-art everything.

"Sure, boo. I even got you some of that grape juice you love, too," he said, biting into another wing. She smiled. He looked like a little boy when he ate. She leaned over and kissed him. She couldn't wait to give him some later.

His cell phone rang, interrupting their conversation.

"Yo, whatsup?" Tyrell said, holding the phone to his ear.

One by one, wrinkles grew on his forehead. And when Tyrell finally put down his chicken, she knew that their plans for later were off. He snapped the phone shut and pushed his mostly empty plate away.

"What's wrong?" Kanika looked into his angry eyes.

"I gotta take care of some real important shit," he said, taking out a wad of twenties and giving it to her. "This is for you. Get whateva' you need later. I'ma have to call you in a few days."

"What I need this for?" she said, looking at the money. He had given her money before, but never this much.

"Just shop or whateva'. And I'll call you. Whateva' happens, know that I love you." He kissed her on her lips.

That was the first time he said, "I love you." And before she could answer, he was gone like the wind out the front door. To where she could only wonder as she stuffed the money in her bra and finished her meal alone.

Across Brooklyn in the basement of Shine social club on Putnam and Bedford, Tony held an emergency meeting. Everyone was settled on chairs and sofas, while a bad-ass, long-haired chick in shorts up her ass handed out drinks. Tyrell had walked in right in the middle of it. He was pissed he hadn't known about this meeting earlier. He was number two and he knew everything, even before Tony. Tyrell couldn't hold his anger at all the bullshit he was hearing. Tony was going on endlessly about killing all the Columbians, this time. Running up in niggas' homes, killing their wives and kids, all to scare them completely away from his territory. He hoped that this would send a message to Cee-Lo's crew that Tony and his people were no one to fuck with. He was gonna take it to the top. Fuck dealing with underlings.

"I thought about it, capping Cee-Lo's peeps don't mean shit if those Columbians just move in when they move out. We need to bury them Spanish niggas, and once they out, it's all for us. No one will fuck with this!" Tony said, sitting on the edge of the pool table dressed in black slacks, black button-up shirt, and fedora.

Tyrell looked at him in disappointment and Tony

called him out, "Yo, nigga, what the fuck is the problem?"

Tyrell calmly approached the center of the room as everyone whispered to themselves. Whatever Tony was thinking was written all over the scowl in his face. He looked like he couldn't wait for Tyrell to say some dumb shit to put his ass on blast in front of everyone. That had happened only once, when he was fifteen, and new to the game. But that had been the first and last time.

"Yo, with all respect, Tony, that's some crazy shit you talkin'. Them Columbians can cut off everybody's motherfuckin' supply. We can't go acting crazy. We need a plan, we need discipline. Discipline is the only way to survive in this game," Tyrell said, both arms folded in front of him. He stood face-to-face with Tony and the murmurs in the room sounded like it was about to be on. No one challenged Tony like Tyrell.

"So you saying *I* don't know how to survive? Nigga, I was in this game when you was still sucking your mama's titties," Tony said, with half a grin. Then he pressed his hands together. "You trying to tell an old nigga like me how to do my shit? You here because of *me*. You got what you got because of *me*. You need to recognize. All you niggas in here do!"

"And we could all do twenty-five to life because of you. And we can all die because you don't know how to keep clean," Tyrell said, toe to toe with Tony.

It was as if they were the only two in the room.

The silence was deafening except for the sound of the bass thumping upstairs in the lounge. "Nigga, say what you gotta say," Tony said, with a snicker. "I got some money to make."

This was it. Tyrell didn't care what the fuck was about to happen. "*Paper, cake, bread,* Tony. Remember that shit? Violence just brings on more violence. It don't bring in more money. This is a business. This ain't no fucking playground for you to fuck with somebody because you don't like niggas. All that shit you was kicking earlier, that's just gonna bring more heat, more attention to our black asses." Then he turned to everyone in the room. "You motherfuckas gonna sit here and let this motherfucka take us down?" Everyone immediately cast their eyes away, some shook their heads in agreement. "Fuck that! I ain't ready to go down for no one!" And feeling ten feet tall, he faced Tony and said, "Not even for you."

Tyrell's tone was filled with so much contempt that Tony's skin turned purplish-red. He stood there like somebody had just stripped him of everything he had—respect.

"I like you, Tyrell," Tony finally said, putting both hands on Tyrell's shoulders. Then he whispered in his ear, "But life without power is intolerable."

No one in the room said anything, but Tyrell could tell by the looks on their faces that they were scared to death. And fear spelled weakness. *Where there's weakness, there's betrayal,* Tyrell thought.

Tyrell knew any moment he could be taken out because there was like fifty cats behind him. But he was willing and ready. He believed in only one man, and that was himself.

Six

A whole day had passed. Kanika hadn't heard from
Tyrell, which was unusual. He would have called
at least three times under normal circumstances.
Kanika flipped the TV channels in her bedroom and
fantasized about her day with him yesterday. They
had gone to church, and she had made a couple of
street runs with him in his car before they went to
Ruthie's. Kanika ravaged her brain for any sign of
something she could have said or done wrong. She
thought that maybe Tony had gotten to him, but he
would have told her right then and there that it was
over. There was something else going on, she thought,
and it had to do with the streets. She wanted to ask
her mother, but like all mothers, Waleema would
just try to protect her. She needed to know the real
deal.

"Peaches, you got a minute?" Kanika asked as
she twirled the phone cord around her hand. Peaches

was Kevin Lyons's girlfriend, and if anyone knew something, she would.

"Yeah, girl, always for you. I have been meaning to call your ass." Peaches sounded like she had something important to say.

"Good, because I need to know what the fuck is going on. I was with Tyrell yesterday and he was acting normal and then he gets this call and the nigga just bounced on me. I haven't heard from him since."

"Girl, Kevin must be with 'im. The block is hot now. As a matter of fact, all them niggas is hot. From what I heard, they supposed to be sitting down with Cee-Lo's people."

"Is that right? I bet they was talking about that shit at my party. Niggas looked too tense," Kanika said, recalling that evening.

"Well, they supposed to get his people to work with Tony and Tyrell's people to push their work all over the Bronx."

"Tony and Tyrell don't know nobody in the Bronx. That ain't nothing but trouble."

"Well, Kevin told me it was Tyrell's idea to get everybody together to try to build a larger empire. Get Cee-Lo's people to keep their strip and they can get a cut. If that don't work, it was going to be all-out war. Tyrell said he would be counting bodies."

Kanika thought about that. "So you think they met already?"

"I haven't seen Kevin since yesterday. Maybe, maybe not. You know how them niggas get. They disappear with their street shit for days and pop back up like nothing happened. I just want my boo home with at least his other leg."

"I did see him at the party with a crutch. I hope there ain't nothing about to jump off. I just got with Tyrell and I don't want to lose him. Or anybody, for that matter."

"I feel you."

"Look, let me get back to you. I'ma try calling him again."

"Later."

Slowly she began to dial Tyrell's number for the tenth time that day. Her heart began to sink when it went straight to voice mail. She knew something had gone wrong. Kanika flung her cell phone across the room. There was no way she could sit still when all hell might be breaking loose out there.

"What's that noise?" Waleema said, opening Kanika's door. "Girl, you OK?"

"I haven't heard from Tyrell. I think something is going on." Kanika rubbed her eyes. "If you know something, please tell me."

Waleema sat down on Kanika's bed. She was dressed in an orange stretch tube dress. Her mother always looked sexy even if she was lounging in the crib. "Tony is gone, too. All of them seem to be in some meeting. That's all I know and that's all you need to know. What did I tell you about getting involved in your man's street hustle?"

"I'm just concerned."

"There are going to be many days like this. I remember sitting up for weeks waiting for Tony. I didn't even get a call from him. Then one day he shows up. No explanations. Nothing. And I had to trust that. Later he told me that he had to make a run to Virginia and Atlanta. I didn't know where he was."

"So what did you do?"

"I waited. I did things to keep me busy. I figured if the police wasn't calling me, it was all good." Waleema stood up. "And this is the same thing. Let's go get some dinner. I'll wait for you downstairs."

Kanika washed her face and threw on a clean, new outfit. Going out to dinner, she thought, would help ease her mind. She and her mother were in the same boat now, and if Waleema said everything was OK, then it just had to be.

Waleema and Kanika headed to a popular seafood restaurant on the other side of Brooklyn, but the traffic was terrible.

"You wanna go to Junior's instead?" Waleema asked Kanika. "By the time we get to Nicole's, it's gonna be too late and I'm hungry now."

"I guess that's cool," Kanika said. She just wanted to get as far away from the house as possible. She needed to be in a new environment to relax.

Waleema's cell phone rang. "Oh, I hope this is Tony," she said, pulling over.

"Yeah, whatsup?" Waleema said when she picked up.

Kanika watched her mother anxiously. Waleema just kept nodding, but from the expression on her face she looked like she was about to kick somebody's ass in.

"What happened?" Kanika asked as soon as her mom hung up. She wondered why Tyrell hadn't called her.

"That was Tony, honey. He's OK. He's at the office. I'ma run over there, before we go to dinner."

"OK," Kanika said, as they sped down Grand Avenue. She thought Tyrell might be there, too.

In a few minutes, Waleema pulled up to what looked like an abandoned building.

"Can I come?" Kanika asked, getting out of the car, too.

Waleema and Kanika walked up to Tony's office on the second floor. He was seated behind a large, black, battered desk, looking mad as hell, hunched over his desk.

"So what's going on?" Waleema said, her hand on her hip. "You never use this office."

"Hey, Kanika, you OK?" Tony asked, walking around to hug the both of them. "I just wanted you two to be near me. No one knows where I am. Only Tyrell knows about this office."

"How is he?" Kanika asked, staring at Tony intently.

"I haven't heard from him," Tony said, with a dry attitude. "I have a feeling a lot of my partners don't like the way I do my business."

"What?" Waleema said, taking a step back in shock.

"This is the safest place for y'all. Everything is hot now."

"Kanika, can you give us a minute? There's a back room," Waleema said.

Kanika did what she was told and walked to the small office in the back. She closed the door, and she could hear Waleema and Tony bickering. Then she heard her mother crying. A few minutes later, Kanika heard pounding on a door. Kanika panicked and ran to the window. She saw two men with black ski masks enter the building.

"Nika, stay in the room!" she heard her mother call out to her. Just when Kanika was about to come out, a shot rang out. Kanika looked through the peephole.

Suddenly she heard a spray of gunshots. Kanika hit the floor, her arms over her head. It sounded like the world was exploding all around her. Then just as suddenly everything went deathly quiet. Kanika slowly lifted her head and listened. Nothing. Carefully she got up, her legs trembling.

Kanika walked into the room just as two men ran in and riddled it with bullets. She ducked behind an office sofa while Waleema and Tony shot back. Tony's bloody body fell over on the desk. Waleema ran toward him and held his lifeless body in her arms. One of the gunmen lay on the floor clutching between his legs, where he'd been shot.

Kanika couldn't believe what she was witnessing. Her mother's clothes were covered in blood.

"Tony! You killed Tony!" Waleema cried, dropping her gun.

"Who else is here, bitch?" one of the gunmen said, as he picked the gun up that lay beside her.

He cocked his gun and pressed it into the skin of Waleema's neck.

"Bitch, you dead!" He was a little over six feet and seemed nervous.

"No!" Kanika shouted, running up on him. "Please don't kill my mommy!"

"Nika, no, honey, no—"

"Shut the fuck up!" he said, chewing on his lips. He didn't seem concerned with Kanika at all.

"Listen, if you wanna kill me, do it," Waleema told the gunman. "But please, don't hurt my baby. She's all I have."

"You better believe she all you got. But just in case." He shot Tony again in his head. "Nigga really dead now." He laughed.

"I should fuck you and your bitch-ass daughter." He ran the mouth of his gun up Waleema's dress and put Kanika in a choke hold.

Kanika saw the other gunman a few feet away, losing consciousness. He was still bleeding profusely from between his legs. She had it all in her mind to go for his gun and clip the men before they clipped her and Waleema, but she could barely breathe in this nigga's grip.

"Get up, bitch," the gunman said. He stuck the gun in Waleema's back and led her to the couch. He flung Kanika to the couch and taunted them with his gun.

"I'ma fuck you while your daughter watches. Maybe she may want to join in." He grinned, showing a row of yellow, rotten teeth. He pushed Waleem's dress down with his gun.

"Don't move, bitch!" he said to Kanika, as she got wind to get the other gunman's gun, which was out of his sight. "I want your ass right here watching your ho-ass mama."

Kanika sat down. The gun was right by her feet. For a moment she met her mother's eyes. Waleema knew about the gun and she was telling her to kill this nigga. No matter what happened she had to take this motherfucker out.

The gunman unzipped his pants and laid his heavy body on top of Waleema. He tried to suck on her titties but Waleema wasn't having that. He hit her in the face so hard, it knocked her unconscious.

That was when Kanika dove for the gun, but before she could raise it and pull the trigger, she heard two shots ring out. She looked up in shock and saw the gunman, standing over her mother, dick hanging out and gun smoking. He had shot Waleema in the heart, then in the head at point-blank range. He smirked as if to say "I told you, bitch."

"No!" Kanika screamed; she fired at him several times. He fired back and a bullet grazed Kanika's right thigh. She hit the floor, but then the sounds of faraway police sirens startled him. For the first time in her life she was relieved to hear the police. Though it took a while being a black neighborhood. He jumped out the second-floor window, leaving Kanika with two dead bodies on her hands.

Kanika ran toward her mother's half-naked, bloody body. She hugged her mother and just wanted to drown herself in the blood. She wanted to be dead just like her.

"Mommy, he's gone now. See, he's gone. Please, Mommy, just look at me," she cried. Her mother's eyes were rolled to the back of her head. "Mommy, I'm sorry!"

She looked at Tony and couldn't stomach it any longer. *Why didn't Tyrell protect us?* Her head began to spin and a dizzy feeling came over her as she fell to the ground.

An hour later, she was lying in a hospital bed, with Tyrell, Peaches, and Chantal by her side.

Seven

The three longest, darkest days in Kanika's life had passed. Chantal, Peaches, and Tyrell helped her with the funeral arrangements. Her mother and Tony were buried the same day. Despite the hundreds of people they knew, Kanika only wanted their closest friends and neighbors to attend.

"The Lord is my shepherd, I shall fear no evil . . ." began the reverend, and the others repeated the words.

The funeral was outdoors on a sweltering August morning. Kanika was locked in Tyrell's embrace, a black veil over her face and a picture of her mother and Tony in her hand. Tyrell's black suit was as dark and solemn as his mood. He had been by her side since he picked her up from the hospital. He had been her rock. She sat slumped over on her wooden chair, as Waleema's and Tony's lacquered mahogany coffins were lowered into the ground.

"Ashes to ashes, dust to dust," said the reverend as he gracefully bowed his head in prayer.

The sounds of soft, anguished crying filled the air as, one by one, people paid their respects. Tyrell held Kanika close and led her to the coffins. She dropped a rose into the ground. "I love you. Bye, Tony, bye, Mommy," she said, her voice cracking. She turned away and her knees buckled. Tyrell grabbed her and kept her from falling, but the look on his face was so tormented that she found herself holding him right back. There were times, over the past three days, when she thought he suffered just as deeply as she did. Carefully she straightened, and Tyrell walked her back to her seat.

As he sat beside her and the minister said the final prayer, she heard Tyrell whisper, "I'm sorry, Lord."

Kanika couldn't hear any more, as her focus was on what she had lost. She knew that Tyrell felt guilty about her mother's and Tony's deaths on his watch.

"Girl, if I can do anything else for you, please let me know," Peaches said as she and Kanika sat in Waleema and Tony's bedroom. Peaches helped Kanika fold up her mother's clothes.

"You and your mama have really helped me. I couldn't thank you enough. I got the horrible part over with the lawyer yesterday. Tony left me his home and anything that belonged to him and my mama. It was like he knew he would die soon. I just got to know what really happened." Kanika stuffed a box full of Waleema's expensive shoes. They wouldn't fit her, so she was giving them away to Goodwill. "You spoke to Kevin?"

"All he told me was that it was Cee-Lo's people and something had gone wrong. Something really bad that caused them niggas to flip."

Kanika sniffed her mother's white cashmere turtleneck. It carried her scent from months ago. She put it in another box. "Well, they probably just getting us back because Tony clipped Cee-Lo."

"It's not that simple. Kevin said that they never had that meeting because Tony called it off and got motherfuckas mad. Tyrell was pissed, too. Niggas was flippin' on Tony, even his own people."

Kanika rubbed her eyes. "Did Kevin say anything about Tyrell?"

"They was all gone; Tony was on his own that night. That is all I know. I swear Cee-Lo's niggas is real grimy. Kevin don't even got the full story."

"I'm not gonna rest until I find out exactly what happened," Kanika said, her mouth formed into a lean, straight line of contempt. They quietly went back to filling the boxes as much as they could with Tony's and Waleema's clothes.

After Peaches left, Kanika waited for Tyrell. She looked around her home. She was only eighteen and had a whole four-story brownstone to manage. Her mother's plants sat pristinely under the kitchen window as if they hadn't a worry that their caretaker was no longer there. Her mother's cooking and her boisterous laughter were now only an echo in the back of Kanika's mind. Tony's friends in the backyard playing dominoes and drinking Henny in paper cups were now all gone. She would pay anything now to catch Tony and her mother getting fresh with each other around the house. The life and energy she had grown so accustomed to had been snatched away. She stared at the family photos of her and Tony and realized how empty she felt.

Kanika jumped at the sound of the doorbell.

When she opened the door, she found Tyrell standing before her, looking like he hadn't slept in days. He had bags under his eyes and it looked like he had lost weight.

She buried her face in his chest, feeling his long platinum chain press into her cheek. They didn't let go of each other as Tyrell walked Kanika back inside and kicked the door closed behind them. She could have stood there holding him all night.

"God knows if I could have I would have thrown myself in front of that bullet just because of you," he said, his arms around her slim waist. Tears slipped down his face and she wiped them away.

Kanika hugged him tighter, feeling the strength of his arms as he kissed her.

"Every night I replay what I did that day. How I could do it differently. Maybe if I didn't get my hair cut when I did, things would have changed. I could have looked out," he said, his words choppy, as he held back more tears.

"Tyrell, you can't blame yourself forever," Kanika said, rubbing his shaved head. His grief devastated her even more. She had expected him to take this bad, but every time she thought he was holding it together, he would bring it all back up.

He took out a handkerchief from his back jeans pocket and wiped his face. "We gotta talk, yo. Have a seat," Tyrell said, his voice tense.

Kanika sat down by the elongated fish tank in the living room and just stared at him, mystified. She was so sure he was going to tell her to move in with him or that he'd move in with her. "Please, Tyrell, just hold me. I just need you here wit' me, baby, please—" Kanika's shoulders shook and she put her face in her hands as she fought to hold back her tears.

Whatever Tyrell was about to tell her had escaped him. He knelt down before Kanika, kissed her forehead, then brushed her lips with his. Hungrily, desperately, Kanika leaned into him as they kissed the way they had the very first time.

"Please, Tyrell, make love to me. I just wanna feel safe again," Kanika begged softly as he pulled down the gold straps to her green tank top. His lips brushed and sucked on her naked shoulders, the tops of her breasts, before returning to her lips. He sucked on her tongue and explored every corner of her mouth with his.

"I want you, too, baby. But we gotta talk first," he

said, clutching her shoulders. "I gotta send you to Virginia."

Kanika sat up straight. "Da hell?"

"Look, there's a hit out on you. Cee-Lo's people was the ones who clipped Tony and Waleema. One of them cats is bent on you joining them. It's gonna get real nasty up here. Police everywhere, yo. There's no discussion about it," Tyrell said, his eyes intensely focused on her. "You have to go."

"But my father . . . I don't even talk to him," Kanika shook her head adamantly. "I got a half sister I barely know."

"Look, you said you got accepted to Hampton, right? School starts in a couple of weeks." He pushed a strand of hair behind her ear.

"Tyrell, I had planned to take a semester off to give me time to get used to my mother being gone. I can't concentrate on school now!"

"You think Waleema would want you to miss even a day from school because of this? You know when it comes to school your mama did not play. You should start on time for her," he said.

Kanika just couldn't believe her ears. Just when she needed him in her life, he was pushing her away. "Why are you doing this? I can handle myself. If I'm away I can't find out what really happened."

"I promise," he said, sitting beside her, "I'ma be right here, checking on the house every day. I'll get down to the bottom of things. I just don't want what happened to your mother to happen to you.

The least I can do for your mother is protect you by all means necessary." He held her face firmly in his hands. "I swear, I don't know what I would do if those motherfuckas got to you, Kanika."

"Are they coming after you, too? Tell me what really went down." Kanika's eyes pleaded with him for any answer to soothe her pain.

Tyrell exhaled noisily. "Well, you know Tony got Cee-Lo clipped. We was supposed to all have a meeting, but Tony canceled it at the last meeting. I told him not to!" Tyrell angrily called out. "Then Cee-Lo's people put a hit out on Tony. Your mama wasn't supposed to be in it. She just got caught in the middle. And *that* I hate that nigga for."

"Who? Tony?"

Tyrell sighed. "Nah, I mean Cee-Lo." He looked away.

"I'm just confused. Last I heard, things were OK. Things were quiet—" Kanika was at a loss for words.

"It's usually quiet before the storm." Tyrell's eyes softened. He stroked her cheeks. "Get in touch with your father and let's get it crackin'. You'll hear from me every day. I promise."

Kanika nodded and looked up at him. There was one question he didn't answer. "Where were you when Tony and my mama was killed?"

"I was looking for him. I didn't know where he was," he said.

But Kanika remembered Tony saying that only Tyrell knew about his secret office spot. "But—"

Tyrell put his finger over Kanika's lips. "I'm taking Tony's spot. It's all about me now up here. Niggas need me," he said, pointing to himself. "Once I get this Cee-Lo shit in order, which is basically cleaning up Tony's mess, the money will start rolling in again like clockwork. Except this time things is gonna be done right."

Kanika frowned. "What you sayin'?"

"Let's just say Tony had a lot of enemies. Niggas didn't like how he was handling his shit. I'm just gonna be real with you—" Then he stopped.

Kanika frowned in confusion. "I always felt that you stopped respecting Tony."

"What?" Tyrell said, standing up. "That nigga may have tried to keep me from you, he may not have been the best negotiator, but we was a team. I look out for my team. Even if we don't always agree."

Kanika gazed into Tyrell's eyes. She wanted to believe every word. He squatted down in front of her and took her in his arms. "I'll never hurt you, Kanika," he said in that deep, smooth voice of his. And that was all she needed to breathe.

After Tyrell put Kanika on the plane the next morning, he filled the gap in his heart at the church. He sat in the last pew. He felt he was too tainted, too bad to sit close to the altar. He prayed for Kanika and their families, and he prayed for himself. He begged for understanding, but then he surrendered. He got down on his knees in his pew, face down with his hands folded against his forehead, and said, "I'm sorry." He cried, alone, and prayed that the darkness would swallow him whole.

Eight

Kanika's father, Shon, was one of those cats who were considered to be from the old school, even though he wasn't even forty yet. He had lived in Virginia most of his life and seen the game from the beginning. It was a big difference from New York, where the violence was ruining the business. Also, the game in New York was now run by only a handful of heads, like Tyrell, because of death and jail. The farther south one went, the harder cats had to work to push their "work." Shon's mules in New York pushed the work through the Greyhound to arrive in Virginia and were under Shon's control and he quadrupled the price that New York cats would charge. In Virginia, the product was harder to get, so cats were ready to pay anything. This was how Shon flourished. He was "da man" in all of Virginia, and everyone came to him when they needed food. He supplied his mules, and they would bring back the bread. He never uttered the words "murder" or "kill" and touched none of the work. He was always clean and no one had access to him outside of his lieutenant Saliq.

Most of his time consisted of long meetings with Saliq, calls to his Mexican cartel, counting his green, or dealing with little issues like the FBI, which would arise every now and then when they got a lead. But nothing ever stuck to Shon. Unfortunately, he couldn't say the same for the rest of his capos, some serving twenty-five to life for drug trafficking.

Kanika hadn't seen Shon in years. As she waited in the airport, she wondered how much his looks had changed. She remembered he was a man who stood out with his powerful six-four stature. She had his chocolate brown skin and high cheekbones. Most of her memories of her father were a blur because Waleema had left him when Kanika was six. Her mother used to complain to her friends and even to her that Shon wanted to keep her under lock and key. And before they killed each other she left and came to New York toting Kanika on her hip.

Kanika smiled to herself at a memory of her mother with both hands on her hips screaming at Shon about running around with some ho and being late with her money. Guess which one she cared about the most? "Nigga, that ho musta sucked your brains out ya dick for you to come up in here without my money! You better take yourself back out in them streets and get my cheese! And next time my money gets fucked up, I'm gonna cut you and that bitch you be with. No questions asked, nigga." No matter what Waleema's past, Kanika would always have a respect for her that no man could compete with.

"Kanika."

She turned around and nearly gasped when she saw her father standing before her. He appeared almost like an angel, wearing a cream-colored linen suit. As she looked at him standing there, her own personal warrior from heaven, tears filled her eyes. This was the way daddies were supposed to look when their little girls were in trouble.

"Hey, baby," her father said, opening his arms. Kanika happily walked into his comforting embrace, forgetting that she hadn't paid for her candy. It felt good to be in his arms, to be with someone she actually shared blood with, she thought. It surprised her, since she had been sure she was gonna give him attitude.

"Hi, Daddy." Kanika looked into his smiling eyes and for a moment wished that he had always been in her life. Maybe he could have protected them better than Tony did. *If only,* she thought.

"Aw man, baby," her father said, taking her bags as they walked out of the terminal. "I am so sorry that you have to go through this. When I heard about your mama, I nearly lost it myself."

"You did?" Kanika said, struggling to hear him above the airport intercoms. "So why didn't you come?"

"I have a business, Kanika, and that is the life I chose. But I wanted to be there more than anything," he said, glancing at her.

A shiny black Escalade waited for them outside. Kanika lifted the hem of her long peach-colored Armani summer skirt and stepped inside the spacious SUV. But not before she peeped at the deliciously chiseled brother at the steering wheel who was checking out every point on her body through the rearview. His platinum adornments shimmered under the sun. Kanika thought her heart had stopped beating at the prowess his eyes commanded. Her father got in beside her. He sat back and allowed his eyes to slowly peruse her.

"Damn, you look more like your mama the older you get. You are just beautiful," he said, then leaned forward and kissed her cheek. "I'm gonna protect you, Kanika. You won't have a need for *anyone* else."

Kanika cut her eyes away from the strange quiet man in the driver's seat. He kept glancing at her in the rearview mirror.

"Yo, Saliq, this my baby girl back here, Kanika. Say whatsup, man," Shon said, feeling some of the chemistry between them.

"Whatsup?" Saliq said, and nodded in the mirror.

Kanika flashed him a brief smile, then quickly looked away.

"OK, now, enough of the formalities. I'm so happy to see you, baby," Shon said, massaging Kanika's arm. "Your skin even feels smooth like

your mommy's." He seemed transfixed by her re-
semblance to her mother. She had the feeling that he
was talking to Waleema and not her.

"Daddy, I may look like Mommy, but I am my
own woman," she told him. She did not want him
bringing the issues he had with her mother into their
own relationship. She knew that her father was pos-
sessive and jealous from what her mother had told
her and that was why she had left.

"Nah, baby. I understand. Your old pops just
feels you need to be looked after. That nigger your
mother was with was a sorry-ass—"

"No, Daddy," Kanika said, shaking her head.
"Tony was more of a father to me than you ever have
been. Let's not get it twisted."

"Hmph," her father said, and they both descended
into silence. Kanika watched the airport get smaller
and smaller through the side-view mirrors. They drove
down the highway to a destination that Kanika knew
little about. They were just a few minutes away from
Hampton Roads, where her mother had grown up.

"You remember living down here?" her father
asked.

"You mean like when I was five? Not really," she
said, giving him a sarcastic look.

"Well, I met your mama when she used to dance
at this spot not too far from where I live now. Don't
worry, Kanika. I got a nice-ass house with anything
you could ever need. And you got your sister waiting
for you, too. She's just a few months younger than

you, so you two can get along like old friends," he said, signaling to Saliq, who had a sarcastic grin on, to lower the AC.

Kanika didn't respond, because she wasn't in any mood to bond. The last time she saw Tiffany was when she was five years old. Kanika hadn't spoken to her since then, even though Waleema tried to get them to talk. "We're all a family," Kanika's mother would say. But when Kanika called Tiffany, she would always be very quiet. And on more than one occasion she told her father she was not there when she was. Kanika thought Tiffany was shady and just hoped that eighteen years had done the same thing for Tiffany's maturity as it had for hers.

"I still can't stand her mama, though. She turned herself into a real crackhead," Kanika's father said, shaking his head. He lit a cigar and rolled down the window.

"Thanks to you, I'm sure," Kanika mumbled under her breath.

"Ay, you listen to me," he said, pointing his finger at Kanika. "I may not be your favorite person, but I'm still your daddy. And I don't appreciate your little attitude."

"Sorry." Kanika sighed as she looked at the rolling Virginia hills outside her window. She didn't mean to be disrespectful and felt embarrassed. One thing her mother told her was to always respect her father, no matter what wrong shit he did.

Her father reached over and turned her face toward him. "Listen, Kanika. There's a lot about your mama and me you don't know. But one thing I can say is that I loved her more than any other woman I've ever met. But she disappointed me. She lost her loyalty and faith in me," he scoffed, his face showing discontent.

Kanika took a deep breath. "What do you mean?"

Her father blew his cigar smoke out the window. "Baby, one day we'll sit down and talk. But know this. Loyalty is why I am alive today. To roll with me you gotta prove your loyalty or pay the price," he said, his eyes hard like stone.

"What about love?"

He laughed gently. "The Bible says a man's own enemies are in his house. *I love loyalty.* And anybody who rides with me dies with me. Now that's some motherfuckin' love. Your mama ain't never get down for me," he said, looking at her. "Are you any different?"

Kanika didn't feel she had to answer that. She turned her attention back to the green pastures of the countryside outside her window. She didn't even listen to her father and Saliq start talking about all the new work they got coming in the next few weeks. Just like she had to earn Shon's loyalty, he had to earn hers, too.

Then when silence occupied the car, Shon made a point of saying to Kanika, "I'ma find who killed your mama. *My* loyalty never dies."

◆ ◆ ◆

About forty minutes later, the SUV pulled up to a colonial-style white house with a long front porch surrounded by a green lawn and sprawling back-yard. Kanika tried to act like she wasn't impressed, but with each step they took to the door her chest pounded.

"What about my bags?" Kanika said as she fol-lowed her father into the house.

"Saliq got them, baby. I guess you ain't used to the royal treatment. He's someone you may want to get to know," Shon said, putting his arm around her.

"I am used to royal treatment. Mommy and Tony made sure I had everything. We drove our own cars," she said, as they walked up the steps.

"Maybe that's what those New York ballers do. But in the dirty-dirty we got our own way of doing things. And I keep my profile low. Can't be seen be-hind the wheel all the time."

"I guess," Kanika said, observing the tranquil-lity and peace of her new surroundings. The birds were chirping happily and she even saw a rabbit run behind a tree. The blueness of the sky was wide and open, with hanging puffy white clouds. This was not what she was used to whatsoever. She wanted to hear the music from the Jeeps driving by, the kids playing outside, the police sirens from miles away.

Kanika's chest felt tight because she didn't know what to expect. She just wanted to be with Tyrell in bed, on her back, calling his name. Going through all these changes was too much, she thought.

Just as Shon reached to insert the key in the door, it was flung open. Tiffany held the door open. She studied Kanika as she and her father walked in.

"This is Kanika. Say hi to your sister, ma. I gotta make some calls." And with that, Kanika's father disappeared behind the French doors.

Kanika surveyed the white venetian blinds, white Italian leather sofas, off-white throw rugs, and cheetah-print pillows. There was a huge oil painting of her father hanging across from the flat-screen TV in the sunken living room. He was seated in a chair, smoking a cigar. The black and gold colors of the painting were dark, daunting, and intimidating, and he looked majestic. Everything in the house looked flawless, from the crystal chandeliers to the spic-and-span mirrored walls and bay windows. But even with all that, she believed what she had in Brooklyn was just as tight.

"Girl, you remember me, right?" Tiffany said, showing off a gold tooth when she smiled. Her hair had blocks of red highlights and was in a short pixie cut.

"Yeah, how you doin'?" Kanika said, as she stood uncomfortably in the foyer.

"Girl, you aight? You looking all around like you lost." Tiffany smiled. "Come on in the kitchen."

Kanika followed her and sat down at the kitchen island.

"You want somethin' to drink?"

"Some juice is cool, thanks," Kanika said, watching Tiffany prance back and forth in a pink fitted Baby Phat short and top set that showed off her thick legs. Kanika automatically felt that Tiffany had missed out on her good daddy genes and must have gotten her mama's. Tiffany's legs were long, but her torso was short and stocky, and her behind didn't have that weight to it like her own did. Tiffany's nose was wide and sat on her face like a big stamp. She just looked like an average girl. Kanika relaxed. She was definitely the dime up in this piece. No competition.

"Here you go," Tiffany said, handing her a glass of what looked like cherry Kool-Aid. She sat down across from her and popped her gum loudly. "So I bet you met Saliq?"

"Who?"

"Saliq. He just drove you and Daddy here. He is Daddy's main man, and his paper is long for days. Ain't he fine?" Tiffany said, blowing a big bubble between her lips.

"He aight," Kanika said, trying to sound bored. She had a man, but Saliq wasn't bad eye candy at all.

"That's it? Well, just so you know the haps, I got dibs on that dick," Tiffany said, bursting another bubble.

"Look, I got my man already." Kanika closed her eyes and prayed that Tiffany would be gone once she opened them. *This is gonna be drama,* she thought, *living with her.*

"What's up with the long skirt? Is that how you New York chicks dressing these days?" Tiffany asked, all up in Kanika's face as she drank her juice. Tiffany laughed and blew up a big bubble of gum.

"My mama was killed. I'm not exactly in the mood for dress-up." Kanika looked down into her drink, a thread of annoyance in her words.

"Oooh, girl, that's right. I am so sorry. That's a shame, what happened to your moms." Tiffany pursed her lips. "I completely forgot."

Kanika tried not to jump out of her chair and knock Tiffany on her country ass. She didn't expect her loss to be that important to Tiffany, but saying that she forgot was some cold shit.

"So what you plan to do out here?" Tiffany asked, unaware of her near miss with a smackdown.

"I start Hampton in a few weeks." Kanika spotted her father in the backyard through the window. He was pacing back and forth as he spoke into his cell. He looked upset.

"School?" Tiffany laughed. "Please, I have to do my last year of high school over again. My dumb-ass teacher is hatin' on me 'cause I be flossin' all da new shit, even though Daddy said he would pay for everything if I go to college."

Kanika couldn't believe that Tiffany had flunked her last year of high school. Waleema had been down in her throat if she even slipped a grade or two away from an A. "Well, I got a scholarship. So it's free for me. Do you work?"

"Well, good for you," Tiffany said sarcastically. "But I don't have to work. If you stay down here long enough you gonna meet some brothas who is gonna wanna take care of you. They will keep you laced in the finest things. School will just get in the way. But real niggas like Saliq don't deal with you college girls."

"Well, I like school and my own money. Any man I am with has to believe in education. I ain't about to put my life in no nigga's hands," Kanika said. She wondered, if her mother had taken control of her own life and not counted on her father or even Tony would she still be alive?

A devilish grin spread across Tiffany's face. "We'll see about that. You just might find that it's another world down here, girl."

Nine

A couple of days passed while Kanika tried her best
to feel part of the family. She had her own room, her
own bathroom, and her father gave her a brand-new
Lexus SC300 to sport. Tiffany was always out, and
their father always had some "business meeting" to
attend. But Tyrell had called Kanika every day like
he promised, and that helped her loneliness. At night
she'd wait up until she got his call on her cell, and
throughout the day it was the same thing. Things were
still hot, he told her, and it was best for her safety if
she stayed put. The more he said that, the more sus-
picious she grew. Was he fucking other bitches?
Was he tryin' to get rid of her? Did he still love her?

She missed Tyrell's body on top of hers, pushing
in and out of her, and their licking each other's
sweat and juices. She missed the smell of his expensive sandalwood cologne in her sheets. One night on

the phone, they had spent almost an hour going over her school plans and their future together.

"I know we gonna have a good life together. You gonna be having my babies; we gonna be living large. Don't ever underestimate how much I love you," he said.

"I love you, too. I be dreaming about you every night fucking me, scolding me, laughing with me. I am so happy that you made it through all the drama. I know we're meant to be together," Kanika said, lying on her side in the dark.

"We one, yo. There is no you or me anymore," he said, his tone heavy. "I'm giving my life to you, Kanika. I know your moms would want that."

"She always liked you." Kanika giggled thinking of her and Waleema in the kitchen the morning after she and Tyrell had sex.

"But sometimes I be wondering what you be doing down there," he said.

"Trying to stop missin' you. I can't wait till classes start. I don't really fit in wit' Tiffany, and my dad is hardly around."

"So what Tiffany do?"

"She dropped out of high school, doesn't work, and she parties all the damn time, even on weeknights," she said, rolling her eyes at the ceiling.

"Hmmm, I see I really gotta get you back here. Just don't go getting mixed up in no foul shit, yo. I'm working hard for us to be together. Understand?"

"Yeah, I do. But I get bored sometimes." Kanika closed her eyes and slipped her hand in her purple satin panties. "I *need* you, Tyrell."

"You know how it goes, baby. In time."

"I want you to fuck the shit out of me so bad," Kanika suddenly burst out.

Tyrell laughed for the first time in a while. "Is that right? What you want me to do, baby?"

Kanika turned on her side and stuck a pillow between her legs. She didn't want to sound too nasty, but now she had opened a can of worms. "I don't know."

"Tell me what you want," he said, that baritone voice vibrating over the phone line into her ear and straight down to her pussy.

"Well . . . I wish you were here, on top of me, slippin' your tongue in my mouth," she said, squeezing the pillow between her thighs.

"Yeah?" Tyrell said with a smile in his voice. "And what else?"

Kanika closed her eyes and lost herself in the memory of their last time together. "Strokin' ya dick in my hot pussy, making it all slippery wet, slapping me on my ass—"

"How about me eatin' that pussy from the back? You know I love me some of that sweet pussy."

"Oh yes, making them nasty slurping sounds, licking up all my cum. *Damn*, Tyrell," Kanika said, throwing the pillow to the ground. She rolled over on her stomach.

"I miss seeing my dick between ya fat lips, suckin' on it like a nasty bitch," he said, his breath getting hard and heavy.

"Mmm, I wish I had that big hot dick in my mouth right now. I could just eat it up." Kanika ground her clit against her fingers, making her whole body into one throbbing ache.

"Tell me what else you want to do."

"I wanna lick dem balls, mmm, mmmm, like this." Kanika made slurping sounds over the phone. She didn't even know what she was doing; all she knew was that she could literally taste his dick at that moment.

"Shit, you gonna make me catch that next plane down there and stab that pussy up like what," he said, lost in his own fantasy, too. "The first thing I want to do is sit you on my face. I want those big-ass thighs all over my face. Then you know I gotta slap that fat ass up—"

Kanika humped her hand until she was swollen with delight. *"Tyrell, Tyrell,"* she panted. "I can't come without you here, baby. Please come down here."

There was silence. Obviously someone got to come.

"Hello?" Kanika said, annoyed. "Tyrell?"

"I'm here. I had to go get some napkins," he said, chuckling. "My shit was backed up for weeks. Damn!"

Kanika smiled; at least she had satisfied him in

that way. But of course it brought to mind other worries. "Tyrell, so how long do you think you can last?"

"Say what?"

"Come on now. None of them gold-digging bitches are stepping to you? What happened to Cee-Lo's ho you was running with?"

"Man, listen. That shit is the past. I'm a man, and if I need some pussy I know where to go."

"That's right; you get your black ass down here. Or send for me and I'll fuck you so hard that you gonna be too tired to think, much less fuck anyone else."

"Chill, yo. I'm saying all this dick is for you. You just make sure my pussy is tight, aight?"

"Don't fuck around with me, Tyrell; that's all I am saying." Kanika smirked. She was sounding so much like her mother, commanding Tyrell's respect.

"Threatening me now?" He laughed. "I see the dick deprivation got you going crazy. Listen, get some sleep."

"Good night, baby," Kanika said, content.

"I'm gonna make you my wifey for real when this is all over."

Kanika closed her eyes again, wondering if she was dreaming his words. "I'm already your wifey. Till death do us part."

It was time for some serious shopping, Kanika thought as she ransacked her dresser drawers. There were only a few days left before her first college class and she didn't want to show up wearing her booty-hugging shorts and dresses. She wanted to look more professional and on-point for her new college experience.

"Where are the designer stores down here?" Kanika asked Tiffany over a grits, bacon, and eggs breakfast in the kitchen nook.

"There's a Saks Fifth Avenue over by Hampton Roads," Tiffany said, biting into a crispy slab of bacon. "One of my boys works there, so I know he'll look out. They got all the hot shit."

Kanika exhaled in relief. "Good God, I wouldn't know what to do without my Louis."

"Well, this is a special kind of Louie. *You'll see what I mean,*" Tiffany said naughtily.

After breakfast, they drove down to Saks with the sunroof open in Tiffany's brand-new gold Jeep Cherokee. It took seconds before Kanika racked up on a pair of Gucci embroidered calf-high boots. The five-hundred-dollar price tag was nothing she even thought about. Looking good was priceless. It would be her fourth pair in the same style.

"Girl, Daddy gave you all that cash?" Kanika asked when Tiffany pulled out a stack of Benjamins from her purse.

"Please. I am too old to be relying on my daddy. I got me some old street player who is sprung off of all this," Tiffany said, smacking her ass. "I never spend my own money, ever."

"To each her own. My mama taught me to look out for myself. Whatever a nigga buys me is because he wants to, not because he has to," Kanika noted, as she tried on the boots.

"That's the dumbest thing I ever heard." Tiffany chuckled, confused by Kanika's slick words.

"If it isn't Tiffany Jones," said a tall, slender, light-skinned brother who looked about forty-five. He had laugh lines around his mouth and a protruding belly despite his slim build. He was dressed in black and smiled from ear to ear. Kanika thought that the suit was a disguise for a foul interior. She didn't like the way he stared at Tiffany like she was a chunk of steak.

"Whatsup, Louie, baby?" Tiffany said, as she practically jumped on him. Kanika minded her own business as she modeled her boots in front of a mirror. *He better not be expecting no friendly greeting from me.*

"And who's this? You bringing me something extra today?" Louie said to Tiffany, shaking a reluctant Kanika's hand.

Tiffany whispered in Kanika's ear, "Girl, get anything you want. *Anything.*"

Kanika looked at Tiffany, wondering what she was up to. She and Louie disappeared toward the back of the showroom.

In that case . . . Kanika smiled. She examined a three-hundred-dollar Prada bag and slipped it over her shoulder. "This shit is so fly!" Some customers looked at her with their noses in the air. *But fuck 'em,*

Kanika thought. She continued searching the racks for all the high-priced shit. She thought Tiffany had it all hemmed up. Louie must be giving them a discount.

Kanika picked up a gold bracelet and chain set, dresses, jeans, blouses in Fendi, Chanel, Dolce & Gabbana, DKNY, Moschino, and Iceberg name brands. She definitely planned to show all the Virginia girls what time it was.

Tiffany reappeared with some clothing items in hand, without Louie. "What he give you? New shit they didn't put out on the floor yet?" Kanika said, picking through Tiffany's clothes.

Tiffany snatched them back and laughed. "Since I'm a big girl, he holds all my special sizes. He knows my style," she said, as they stood in line.

"Oh, these are all together, ma'am," Tiffany said to the cashier, as she combined her and Kanika's clothes.

"Where's Louie?" Kanika asked, thinking he had to be around for the discount.

"Code 1030." Tiffany gave the cashier Louie's transaction code. They got his thirty-five percent manager's discount.

"Damn, girl! I heard of looking out, but these clothes are almost half off," Kanika said, thinking she should have bought more things. "Where he at? I need to thank him personally."

The cashier handed them the bags and they walked away. "I did that already," Tiffany said casually.

"He was real nice to do that, because that was some extra shit right there. It means you must be giving him some good business."

"He got his hustle. And I got mine." Tiffany nodded to herself as they put the bags in the trunk.

Kanika smelled more than friendly relations. As they both slid into their seats, she asked, "Did you *do* anything with his old ass to get these?"

"I let him eat my pussy." Tiffany ran her tongue over her glossy lips. "I can pocket the rest of my cheese now."

"That's what I call *real* customer service," Kanika said with cynicism. She couldn't hate on Tiffany for trying to get over but thought she didn't need to give her pussy away for tasting samples. But like she said, everyone had their own hustle.

Ten

On Friday, Kanika and her father returned from freshman orientation at Hampton.

"So baby, tell me again what major you taking up?" her father asked, as they pulled into the winding driveway.

"Economics," she said, slipping on her gold-rimmed Fendi shades that matched perfectly her orange tube top, thigh-high cotton shorts, and sneakers. "I've always loved math and numbers."

"You just like ya mama, girl. She liked her numbers with six zeros or more at the end." He laughed, shooting her a grin. "I might have you come look after your daddy's bankroll."

Kanika and her father got out of the car, and she looked at him to see if he was serious. Shaking her head adamantly, Kanika said, "I can get a job at some kind of financial company. I can get into politics, too."

Her father threw her a bewildered look, as if the thought of her working was alien to him. "Well, that's what you say now."

"Yeah, whateva'," Kanika said, slamming the car door. Her mother had run her own business and that alone was enough motivation for Kanika.

They walked into the house to find Tiffany counting green stacks of bills, all piled up around her like armor.

"Don't be mixing up my twenties and Benjamins like you did the last time," her father said, standing behind her as she counted. Tiffany didn't even look up until she was through. She had the wet sponge out for her thumb to help flip the bills, an apron where she kept extra notepads, and a headset.

She slid her headset off and said, "Whatsup, y'all? I thought I had the whole house to myself today."

"Not when you got over half a million dollars on your mothafuckin' lap," her father answered. And there was more where that came from. His Colombian cartel connect just hit him off with mad bricks and enough food to eat for the rest of the year. Their supply was now doubled because of all the older cats who were leaving the game because of him. New spots that had harbored old crack dens had become crack mansions, with a whole new wave of customers coming to him. He charged them whatever for food, and they did whatever to eat.

Kanika eyed the stacks. She missed being home.

Her mother had always counted Tony's money at night, when everyone else was asleep. Kanika remembered creeping down the steps and just watching her add up thousands and thousands just by looking at them. She rarely used a calculator and never missed a dollar.

"Sit down, girl, you all big eyed. You ain't never seen no money before?" Tiffany said, teasing Kanika, who sat down in front of her.

"T., just keep ya mind on my motherfuckin' money," Shon said as he walked to the refrigerator.

As soon as he turned his back, Tiffany stuck a wad of twenties in her bra and winked at Kanika. Kanika put her hand over her mouth. Tiffany went back to counting like nothing.

"Fuck, T.!" Shon set his glass of Southern Comfort on the counter and grabbed Tiffany by the neck, slamming her down on the kitchen island. "You gonna try and rob me in my own mothafuckin' house!" He stuck his hand down her shirt and dug out the money. Kanika cringed while Shon held Tiffany down like she was a two-dollar street ho.

Red marks from Shon's fingers stood out on Tiffany's light-skinned neck. She held on to her breasts, sucked her teeth, and went right back to counting. It was obvious that Shon had eyes in the back of his motherfuckin' head when it came to his money.

But in minutes Tiffany and her father were both laughing about her stunt at Saks Fifth Avenue.

Tiffany didn't tell Shon what she had to give up, but she explained how she had played Louie and was able to walk away with designer threads while keeping most of her paper. Shon congratulated her on a hustle well done.

Kanika washed off a cucumber facial mask and got ready for her night of beauty rest. Her first classes were in the morning and she was amped. Before she hit the sheets, Peaches called. It had been weeks since she heard from her girl.

"I miss you!" Peaches squealed. "I been wanting to call but wanted to give you a chance to settle in."

"It's good to hear from you, girl. I missed you, too. You workin' or in school?"

"I'm workin'. I need to make my own paper. I got a job where my mom works. She got me being a receptionist until I know what I want to do."

"OK, but you always been smart."

"You the smart one, girl! You got everything." Then she heard the silence. "So how are you feeling?"

Kanika turned off her bedside lamp. "Girl, each day that goes by I love Tyrell more and miss my mama. You know what they say about absence and the heart."

"How is they treating you down there?"

"I feel like nobody really cares what happened to me. No one seemed altered by my mom's death but me. At least back home I could share my pain with

Tyrell. He's really taking it hard. Harder than I thought."

"Speaking of, I heard two of Cee-Lo's boys were shot execution style in the Ocean Hill projects. It's like Tyrell is getting rid of all them. He's really on a mission."

Kanika smiled. "That's my heart."

"A lot has changed," Peaches said, sounding nostalgic for better times. "No more parties; the bus rides to Atlantic City and Mohegan Sun have all been canceled. More flowers and well-wishes on cards are on your doorstep every day. Them boys is everywhere."

"Well, good. I hope they catch them evil motherfuckas. I wish I could kill them my damn self."

"Tyrell's gonna get there before you do. I haven't seen him around much, though. He must be laying low."

"Watch him for me, girl. I know he got needs, like most men. But if I hear of another chick even looking at him, it's gonna get dirty for bitches up there." Kanika could feel her whole body getting tight as she imagined that happening.

Peaches quieted down. It seemed like she was preparing what to say and how to say it. "I know you got Tyrell, Kanika, but everybody need a sidepiece. Then you won't miss him so much."

Kanika couldn't even consider being with someone else and was put off by Peaches just suggesting it. "No man can make up for all the man I have in

Tyrell. Here or there, I would never feel right stepping out on him. I made a promise I'm gonna keep," Kanika said. "Unless he fucks up on me first." She did have to recognize that anything was possible.

"I'm just saying bitches is gonna start checking for Tyrell. He's the head nigga now, giving orders and pulling in mad cheese. Just be aware of all that."

"You actin' like you know he gonna cheat," Kanika said, catching attitude. "Me and Tyrell got a bond. He is too busy making it safe for us again to be out there *dating*. Fuck that."

"I'm not pressing the issue. Just thought I'd put it out there."

"You seen that light-skinned chick who was at Tony's party a few months back? She was with Tyrell at that time."

"Yeah, she be around. But since everything went down, I heard she workin' close wit' the police. So niggas ain't fuckin' wit' her no more."

"Well, watch that bitch. I'm in love, but I ain't no fool."

"He and half the niggas from Brooklyn was messing with that ho. That was before you, though," Peaches said.

Kanika slipped her hands under the pillow for a picture of her and Tyrell she slept with nightly. She kissed it. "And there will be none after me."

"Now that's the Kanika I know. I may be down in VA to see fam' in a few weeks. We should hit up some spots."

"That would be so good! Now I got an excuse to get me out of this house," Kanika said as she peeked out the window and saw her father pull up in their driveway with his new flavor of the week trailing behind him.

"Cool."

"But remember what I said about Tyrell. I'll hit you back later, and tell everyone I'll be home soon."

"Of course. You know I always got your back."

When they hung up, Kanika fell asleep with Tyrell's photo in her hand.

Eleven

It had been well over a month since Tyrell had laid his hands on Kanika. He missed everything about her, from her long eyelashes to her silky smooth body. But there was so much he needed to tell her, so much she needed to know. He had as much blood on his hands as Tony had in all his life by now. Once niggas heard that Tony was dead, Tyrell and his crew became targets. Until they found out that Tyrell was the wrong one to fuck with. He didn't play with guns, he played with words and minds. He made a major deal with Cee-Lo's people and he was able to multiply his paper by claiming their territory. They would work for him, get their supply, and a generous cut. Even the Columbians had to bow down. But Tyrell knew that things were still built on shaky ground.

"I need to talk to you about some wild shit I

heard," Kevin said, sitting down across from Tyrell in his brand-new "office."

"Listen, we need to focus. I just got hit off with some major bread from those Colombian mother-fuckas to push this work through the streets like a five-dollar ho. I wanna get the Gs stacked before them boys catch on. So tell them niggas out in the street to stay clean."

"Got that," Kevin said, nodding. "But that's not what I want to talk about."

"Well, nigga, that's what I want to talk about. This is how we eat. Now you here for business or what?" Tyrell didn't want to have to be so harsh with Kevin, but he had been under some serious stress lately. He was feeling anxious about the heavy burden he carried.

Kevin took his baseball cap off. "This is some important shit. You know Sharnell, Cee-Lo's ex-bitch who you was fucking with for a minute? She supposedly is telling niggas that you clipped Tony and Waleema."

Tyrell's eyes froze on Kevin's face; then he leaned back casually. "That bitch is crazy. Probably mad because I dumped her ass when I got with Kanika. If I catch that bitch in the street—" Tyrell slammed his hand down on his desk.

"That's the thing: nobody know where she is. I would cap that bitch myself. Fuck she come from?" Kevin said, with hatred lacing his words. "If the po-

po catch on to that, it's all over, yo. They gonna be in our asses like hemorrhoids."

"She talked to the po-po?"

"The bitch got a big-ass mouth. She talking to somebody."

"Aight, yo, I need some time alone," Tyrell said, spinning his leather chair around. When he heard the door close, he thanked God Kanika wasn't around to hear these vicious rumors. This would delay her return even more. But he had to take care of this first. It would break his heart if Kanika heard that he had anything to do with Waleema's and Tony's deaths. He knew she would crumble to pieces, but he was strong. He was at a level now where he knew niggas were hatin'. Besides the Bronx, there were no more street hustlers he had to wrestle the money and power from. He was holding down Brooklyn and he wouldn't let anyone get in the way of that.

When he had been just a young one, he had been a teenager making runs for the OGs. Now he was that OG, at twenty-four, at a time when the game had fewer players, due to death and incarceration. A lot of niggas were trying to break into rap as the way out of the hood. But Tyrell preferred the adrenaline rush of street life, the smell of the millions he got in a week's work, and being part of the legendary drug stories that rappers emulated and that made New York City the only place he wanted to be. He envisioned himself as an immortalized icon of the hood.

Kanika was part of that vision. Every hustler had a bad-ass woman. A chick who would die before she ever turned her man in, catch a case for him if she had to, fight to her last breath before she ever let another woman take her place, and, most important, surrender her body, mind, and soul. He had that in Kanika. He wanted to be all those things for her, too. She was his moon and sun and made his life worth living. He saw a future with her that didn't include a life of running and gunning but one where he could have a white picket fence, a sprawling backyard, and a house full of smart kids who went to private school and church on Sunday. He wondered if he could ever be that man for her. Sometimes he hated her just a little for being everything he ever wanted and everything he might never have. He wanted to be that good man, a normal man, but the streets kept calling.

Ring. Ring.

It wasn't Kanika, like he had hoped. "Who this?" he asked, stumped by another woman's unrecognizable voice.

"Tyrell, it's Peaches."

Tyrell stared out his office window and let out a stressful sigh. Peaches had never called him before. "Did something happen to Kanika?"

"Oh no, she's doing good in VA. But you know how she be worried about you," Peaches said.

"Yeah, well, what is it then?"

"I'm in town for the weekend. She told me to check

on your ass because I know how these females around here be."

"Oh, really?" he said, a smile spreading across his lips. Kanika's jealousy always turned him on.

"Well, you know she always take care of her man, and she told me to make sure you eating right."

Tyrell spun around in his chair as Peaches' words rang new to him. "She ain't never tell me that."

"It's a woman thing. Look, my mama made some chicken parmigiana today with spaghetti and she baked a cake. If you ain't too busy, you should stop by."

"I love Italian, but . . ." Tyrell said. He needed some home cooking. Every night he would order out or eat at some fancy restaurant with some of his capos. But . . . "I've got mad work to do. Business."

"Everybody eats. I know you do, as built as you are," Peaches said in a giggly voice. "What my moms made tastes *real* good, too."

"Black folks don't know how to cook Italian." He laughed. "They put too much other shit in it."

"Well, come see for yourself," Peaches said.

"Is your moms gonna be there?" he asked. Something in her voice made him ask.

"Of course, nigga. Don't play me," Peaches said seriously. "My mom will be here and so will I."

Peaches lived near the Fort Greene projects. Her uncle was down with the life until his last day, when he died of cardiac arrest during a police raid. Quaron had a known heart condition, but that didn't stop him from raking in millions back in the day. But since him, Peaches' family had laid low, living off his wealth and hitching their Acuras to Kanika's family's history of long paper and legendary respect.

Tyrell planned to just eat and run, but he didn't want to be rude to Peaches' moms. He rang the bell, and as soon as the door opened, a waft of warm bread, baked chicken, and bubbling cheese led the way. Peaches smiled at him.

Peaches was dark skinned, like Kanika, but her skin wasn't as pretty and even toned. Her hair, which she changed every other week, was now shaved in the back, cropped and spiky in the front. She definitely had some style. Her body was tight, thicker than Kanika's but not as shapely.

"Whatsup, nigga?" Peaches said, giving Tyrell a friendly pound. She was holding a small glass of Henny in her left hand. She waved him in, then led him into the living room.

The living room was cozy, but cluttered. Chips of olive green paint gathered at the corners and at the foot of the radiator. Yellow sponge material stuck out from the bottom of the black leather couch. Dead ferns adorned the windowsill. Tyrell pointed out one good thing. "Smells good," he said, removing his jacket and putting it next to him on the couch when he sat down. "I actually can't hang too long because I got some running to do later."

"I know; I know," Peaches said, taking the last sip of her drink. She plopped down next to Tyrell on the couch. She wore tight blue hip-hugging sweatpants and a cut-off wifebeater that showed the brown of her big, hard nipples.

"Where your moms at?" Tyrell asked, looking around, but he didn't hear anything but the faint sound of a TV in the back. Suddenly he wanted to call Kanika and tell her where he was. "I gotta make a call real quick."

Peaches pulled him back down to the couch. "Uh-uh." She grinned, waving her finger in his face. "My mama went to the store; she'll be right back. I know you ain't thinking no dumb shit."

"Nah." Tyrell laughed. This was Kanika's best friend and he didn't want to embarrass her or himself by suggesting that, but he didn't want to play the back, either.

"She said we can eat whenever; I'm not sure when she's coming back," Peaches said, standing back up and in front of Tyrell. She put her hand on her hip. "Is that OK with you?"

"I'm just ready to eat. A brother ain't had no home meal since, damn, since—" Then he laughed to himself and it eased the discomfort he was feeling.

"Cool. Then come on over here and let me fill your plate. I know Kanika would be so happy that her man is getting fed the right way." Tyrell followed her into the kitchen.

The kitchen looked a bit better. Large, open bay windows let in some summer breeze and sunlight. There was only milk and cheese in the fridge, when Peaches opened it to get out two cans of soda.

While they ate, Peaches yammered on while Tyrell thought about how he missed these moments with Kanika. Just kicking back, doing dumb shit together, anything to forget about the drama out in the world.

After dinner, Tyrell made his move to leave. "Yo, tell your moms thank you. The food was the best Italian I ever tasted. When she makes lasagna, give a nigga a call," he said, grabbing his jacket.

"Damn, Tyrell, swallow the food first before you leave. Come on; just chill. Maybe you can say hi to my moms or something. She should be back soon," Peaches said, following him into the living room. She sat back down on the couch and signaled for Tyrell to do the same.

He sat down across from her. "I'll wait a few. I don't wanna seem rude or nothing, but I got shit to do."

Peaches flipped through the TV channels. "So how you making out with Kanika gone? I know she miss you like hell."

"It's hard. I talk to her more now than I did when she was here. But you know, we gotta do what we gotta do," he said, staring at the tube.

"She meeting a lot of people down there. Any time I talk to her she going to a new party or something.

Plus, she made some new friends. I told her she better not forget about me," Peaches said, unwrapping a red lollipop she took out of her sweatpants pocket.

"You two go way back. So I doubt that," Tyrell said.

"You don't ever think about that? She's living a whole new life down there. I know there are mad niggas trying to get her attention. She told me." She let the lollipop pop out of her mouth.

"She never told me that," Tyrell said, trying not to sound too interested, but he was. Kanika would never forget about him, never.

"Of course, she ain't telling your crazy black ass, but I'm just letting you know. Everybody got needs, Tyrell," Peaches said.

Tyrell tried to ignore her lollipop, but the more he did, the harder she sucked on it. He wasn't about to discuss his personal life with her, but he was boiling inside and he hadn't heard from Kanika all night.

"So, what you been up to?" Peaches asked.

"Living," he said, glad that the lollipop had now turned to gum. "You?"

"I've been working out. Trying to get my body right. Some of us ain't blessed like Kanika," she said, slapping her thigh. She stood up and walked over to Tyrell. "You think I've been working out too much?" she asked. She ran her hand over her hip.

Tyrell studied her. Peaches was giving him those bedroom eyes. She licked her lips and her tongue had a tinge of red on it from the sweet lollipop. He had to look away to stop himself from getting aroused. What the hell was wrong with him? What the hell was wrong with her? Maybe she had put something in his food.

"Feel this." Peaches grabbed his hand and placed it on her ass. "Does it feel too hard, or is it soft enough?"

Tyrell closed his eyes, not wanting to see his hand on Peaches' ass. This girl was slick, he thought. This wasn't supposed to be happening. "You may want to slow down on the StairMaster," he said, removing his hand. But all he could think about was Kanika all up in some nigga's face, while he was up here trying to get things right for him and her.

"And this?" She took his hands and placed them on her breasts. "Too many pull-ups?"

Tyrell stared at his hands on her titties, then he looked up at her. Well, Peaches was here and she was down for whatever. "Yeah, too many," he said, his voice all low and deep. But then he pinched her nipples just hard enough to make her gasp. Peaches pressed his hands over her breasts.

"I know this may not look right, Tyrell, but as far as I'm concerned, as Kanika's friend, I'm doing a duty. If I fuck you, then we both know you don't have to go out there and fuck no stank-bitch stranger," she said, stepping back and pulling off her T-shirt. Her titties looked like juicy pieces of fruit waiting to be plucked. "We keep it in the family. Well, sort of."

She smiled, arching her back. "Suck them for me. Please."

Tyrell leaned forward and allowed his lips, then his tongue, to graze her hard nipple. Then he sucked, pulling until she cried out.

Peaches moaned. "Ooh, I can't wait to fuck you," she said. She got up and pulled off her sweatpants. She didn't have on any panties. "Here." She passed him a condom that was tucked behind the sofa pillow where she planted it.

"Bend over," he said, standing up as he unzipped his jeans. Peaches quickly leaned over the couch with her legs spread open.

With his clothes still on, Tyrell whipped out his dick, slipped on the condom, gripped her toned thighs and slid inside her, and gave Peaches exactly what she wanted. He was relieved he didn't have to see her face; it would have made him go soft in a hurry.

"Ohhh, this dick is too damn good to be alone. Kanika is crazy." She moaned and laughed at the same time.

"Shut the fuck up!" he said, pounding her soaked pussy with all his might. It wasn't long before Peaches came, hard. Cum dripped down her thighs. The harder he pounded into her, the harder she came. It wasn't long before he came, too.

Before he had gone completely soft, he pulled out of her, took off the condom, and buckled his pants.

Peaches turned around and stared at him.

He glared at her like what had just gone down was her fault. "I gotta go."

Peaches slipped on her pants and sat on the couch. "Anytime, I'm right here, Tyrell."

His hands shook as he adjusted his watch around his wrist. The complete awfulness of what had just happened in three minutes overwhelmed him. But he played it cool. "Peaches, this some ole crazy shit you planned, but I'm only a man," he said. He didn't want to get into how she had to keep their secret. It would create some kind of bond that he didn't want to have with her. He didn't want her to feel she could use it against him.

"This was strictly business, Tyrell," she said, winking at him. "I'm leaving for VA on Monday. I'll tell Kanika you said hi."

It relieved him that she would be out of town.

"Thanks for dinner."

"You're welcome."

Tyrell walked out the door, got into his car, and blocked out Peaches and his stomach pains. Just before he went to his bed that night, he called Kanika. They talked for hours about nothing. Her voice soothed him and his sour stomach.

Twelve

The last Wednesday of August was Kanika's first day of classes at Hampton University. She was looking forward to getting into her own routine away from her father's house. Kanika drove alone, even though her father had promised he'd take her. She pictured her mother waiting for her when she got home, wanting a complete rundown of all her classes like she had on Kanika's first day of high school. But she was on her own now. There was no mother to brag about her good grades or smooth out the rough edges in her life. She had to have her own back from now on. It was on her to do her best to make herself happy, and no one else. She wanted to make her mother happy in spirit as she did in the flesh.

At noon, Kanika was sitting in Freshman Composition: Arts and Culture, thinking about how it would be at New York University, where she had also been accepted. Tyrell would pick her up from school; they would go to BBQ's and then back home to make love. But she had to admit to herself that with Tyrell's lifestyle she'd still be doing a lot on her own. Besides to empower herself, she thought, maybe that was why her mama had opened the strip club, to give her something to do. Kanika looked around at the black and brown faces attentively listening to a lecture by an astute gray-haired black professor with thick-rimmed glasses. Rows of green lawn and the lush leaves from trees waved to her from outside the window. There were no police sirens or skyscrapers blocking the view of the cloudless turquoise sky. It was peaceful, and so was she.

After class, Kanika stood in the long, winding line in the school cafeteria waiting to order her Burger King combo when a girl in a red jersey dress that begged her thighs for mercy walked up to her.

"Excuse me, but who does your hair?" she asked.

Kanika looked behind her, not sure if the short but shapely girl was talking to someone else. In New York, people didn't just kick it to anybody like that.

"Your shit is like da bomb. It's so black and shiny. Do you go to Sally & June's?"

Kanika flipped her hair off her shoulders, somewhat happy that someone had spoken to her. "I got it done in New York."

"Girl, it just looks so natural and wavy," the girl said, walking around Kanika, fascinated by her tresses. "Are those D & G jeans?"

Kanika nodded.

"Everywhere I go, they don't have my size." She put out her hand. "I'm Shanae."

"Hi, Shanae. My name is Kanika." Kanika diverted her eyes back up to the menu. Shanae's hair was atrocious, with purple streaks and in an outdated French-roll style with puffy roots. Back home, Kanika thought, she would not be caught dead with a chick like this.

"So," Shanae said, standing beside Kanika. "You new around here?"

"I guess, but aren't we all, since we're freshmen?" Kanika smiled.

"Well, I mean you said you from New York. You got family down here?"

"Yeah, my father, and my sister, Tiffany. She works as a bank teller downtown."

"Tiffany with the gold tooth and pineapple curls?" Shanae shouted, her book bag bouncing on her back. "How she doin'?"

"You know her?" Kanika moved up in the line. Thank God, Tiffany wasn't wearing those pineapple curls anymore, Kanika thought.

Kanika placed her order for a Whopper, fries, and a soda. The way Shanae was looking, it seemed like Kanika wasn't going to have her private lunch talking to Tyrell on her cell.

She paid the cashier and took her order. A few minutes later, Shanae walked over to her table.

"So I know Tiff been taking you everywhere. She

knows everybody, and everybody knows Tiff and her father. Y'all live in that big ole white house on the hill," Shanae said, shaking her head. "I can't believe you her sister." She tapped her chin with her long fake gold nails.

"Why not?" Kanika asked, biting into her burger. Shanae looked like the type who had inside info on everyone. Kanika thought Shanae could just entertain her for the time being.

"I dunno; you just seem nicer, prettier, and she let you hang with her?"

"Let me? If I want to go somewhere, I go. But lately I haven't felt like it."

"Well, the Tiff I know usually likes being the center of attention, especially with the fellas. But I can see you giving Tiff a run for her money. I mean, she cute and all, but I know niggas will be all up in your grill."

Kanika shrugged. "Who knows? I'm gonna be too busy with school to be into all that."

"Look, here's my number. Tiff and I sometimes go to this club called Ambiance. You should roll with us," Shanae said, taking one of Kanika's fries without asking.

"OK," Kanika said, taking the slip of paper. "I'll let you know."

"Girl, let me get going. I have a hair appointment down at Sally's. We should hang this weekend. Call me!" Shanae and her purple French roll walked away with a lively gait.

Kanika finished her food and stared at Shanae's number a few times. She liked her. And if she couldn't get her to change her hair, she'd at least make a nice friend.

Thirteen

When Kanika reached home, she had the house to herself and called Tyrell. He had called her twice on her drive back, but she couldn't answer because she wanted to concentrate on the road. Her worst nightmare was getting lost in some white backwoods town.

"Whatsup, boo-boo?" Kanika said in her most sultry voice when he picked up.

"What's good, yo?" Tyrell said, sounding happy to hear from her. "How was your first day at college?"

"It was cool. The place is nice, really pretty. Nothing like NYU, I'm sure," she said, rolling over on her side in the bed.

"So you meet anybody?"

"Yeah, I met this girl who asked me about my hair and we talked. She seemed nice."

"Oh." Tyrell sighed. "Is that gonna be your new best friend?"

"I don't know, Tyrell," Kanika said with a small laugh. "I mean, we talked; she gave me her number."

Tyrell stayed quiet.

Kanika did, too; she figured Tyrell might be concerned that she'd forget about him. She didn't know what to do to make him think differently.

"You got something on your mind?" she asked quietly.

"What kind of question is that? I got mad shit on my mind, tryin' to protect my neck, my money, you—"

"Peaches told me what was going on."

"She did?" Tyrell asked, covering his face. *Oh, hell no . . .* he thought.

"She said there are flowers and cards outside the house."

"Yeah," Tyrell said, catching his breath. "I'm saving everything for you."

Kanika closed her eyes because of what else Peaches had told her. Fuck it. She had to know. "Are you fucking somebody?"

"What?" Tyrell couldn't take this anymore.

Kanika chewed on her bottom lip. She wanted to keep Peaches out of it. "I know you got needs. Bitches must be all in your face now that I'm gone."

"Come on, now why would I play you like that? Besides, 'nuff bitches got mad respect for you and all you been through," he said, feeling like shit. "What about you? I know you got niggas pushin' up

on you." He sounded like he wanted to murder someone, the volume of his voice increasing.

"Maybe," she said, sounding smug. "But this
pussy belongs to you."

"How I know that?" he demanded loudly.

Kanika sat up in her bed. Tyrell didn't sound
good at all. She thought this was supposed to be
about his dirt, not hers.

"You doing good down there, making friends, next
thing I know you gonna have some motherfucka in
my pussy."

"Tyrell!" she shouted, cutting off his rant. If she
was there with him, she knew it would've gotten real
ugly.

"I'm just saying, anything is possible."

"Tyrell, why are you playing fuckin' mind games
with me? Why don't you just come down here and
see for your damn self? I'm basically alone."

"I know you are; that's why anything is possible."

"You know what? I don't need this bullshit. Are
you trying to leave me like my mother did? By myself?" Kanika began to tear up.

Tyrell was immediately contrite. "Nika, calm
down. Listen, I'm sorry—"

"Fuck you!" she said, and threw her cell across
the room. It shattered into pieces against the wall.

Kanika threw herself down on her bed, burying
her face in her white satin pillow, and had the hard-
est cry she'd had since her mother's death. She
didn't care who heard her. She hated Tyrell for mak-

ing her feel guilty for nothing. She wanted to hop in her car and drive the miles to see him at this very moment. She wouldn't argue with him but ask him to hold her and make love to her. She missed him no matter how much he pissed her off. She loved him, and it was too late for her to undo that just because of a petty argument. Maybe his attitude was Tyrell's way of dealing with his loss of her and missing her, too.

There was a knock on her bedroom door.

Kanika pulled the covers over her head. She didn't know anybody was in the house. She was yelling so loud on the phone, it didn't cross her mind. She prayed they'd take a hint if she didn't answer. *It's probably nosy-ass Tiffany anyway,* she thought.

They knocked again.

"Come in," Kanika huffed, curling up in the bed, like she was asleep.

"You aight?" her father asked, standing at the doorway in jeans and a basketball shirt. "I heard all that yelling, crying, and that big-ass bang. What happened?"

"Nothing," Kanika said, her voice muffled by the covers.

"Was that your *boyfriend* on the phone?" her father asked, his expression curious, as if the thought of Kanika having a man in her life never occurred to him.

Kanika nodded.

"He from New York?"

"Yeah," Kanika said, wanting to be left alone in her misery.

"What's his name?"

"Why?"

"I'm sure the boy got a name. Don't he?"

"It's Tyrell."

"That the cat who ran with Tony? Instead of chitchatting with you on the phone, he should be findin' out who killed Waleema. I know I am."

"He's working on it," Kanika said, not sure where her father was going with this. He had never met Tyrell as far as she could remember, but her father knew all about the man who had replaced him in Waleema's life.

"Well, if you need me to set that mothafucka straight—he threatened you?"

"No, Daddy!" Kanika said, frustrated with everyone jumping to conclusions on her today. She threw back the covers. "We had an argument, like people do when they're together. He's good to me. We're fine."

"I just don't know how a nigga like that ain't catch them mothafuckas yet. If I was up there—" Shon said, his expression murderous.

"But you wasn't!" she said, throwing the covers off and sitting up. "Tyrell is only one man. And he was good to me, and Mommy. Where was you at when niggas was backing my moms down and had the heat to her head?"

Shon stood in the door way for a few more seconds in silence before he turned and left. A feeling of discomfort came over her. He was just too interested in Tyrell, and if he wanted to, Shon could make an already bad situation worse.

Fourteen

Kanika had bought a new cell phone the following day and text-messaged Tyrell her new number, but he hadn't called yet. It was just her second day of school and she already had assignments due the following week. Usually she'd be excited to delve into a new project, but not this time. The last few months had been a whirlwind, depleting her of her energy and drive. The good news was that Peaches was in town. It was a Thursday night, and Kanika needed a release.

She remembered that Shanae had told her that Ambiance was "da spot," and one of Peaches' cousins confirmed that it was the place to see or be seen. It was where all the hustlers went when they needed to find a chick to spend some money on. When she and Peaches got there, they walked up to the line and found Tiffany and Shanae in the middle of the crowd.

"What? You stalkin' me now?" Tiffany laughed as she stood by Shanae, who wore a blond blunt-cut weave that made her look straight out of a Mary J. Blige video circa 1993. Peaches and Tiffany wore short, tight-fitting stretch spandex dresses with heels that lasted for days. But Kanika looked like she had a style and mind of her own in a simple gold and white bodysuit with a V-neck that dipped down past her breasts, and an elegant gold sash that accentuated her tiny waist.

"Please, I'm here with my girl," Kanika said proudly. "Peaches, this is Tiffany, my half sister," Kanika said, sounding like the word "sister" took too much effort. "And Shanae."

"Oh. Don't tell me you from New York, too?" Tiffany asked rolling her neck.

"Yeah, and?" Peaches said with equal attitude.

"Nothing; it's all good," Tiffany answered. But Kanika could tell by her phony grin that Tiffany was trying to start something.

"I ain't about to wait on no line to get in a club. Never have, never will," Kanika said to Peaches and Tiffany. "I'm ready to hop back in the car and head someplace where I get treated right."

"Wait now; we was just about to go in. Come with us." Kanika and Peaches followed Tiffany and Shanae. They skipped anxious partygoers waiting for their turn to enter, and marched their way up to the bouncer.

"Hey, Trey, we all together," Tiffany said, ignoring Peaches.

Trey unlocked the velvet rope and let them through, except Peaches.

"See, I bet you thought I was some ole country bamma. I got connects all up in here," Tiffany said. When Kanika turned around, she noticed that Peaches was still outside.

"Tiffany, if Peaches can't get in, I'm out," Kanika said, irritated by Tiffany's slick move.

"Damn! I can't just be letting in whoever."

"She's not 'whoever'; she's my best friend," Kanika said, about to regulate on somebody's ass.

Tiffany aimed a piercing look at Peaches and whispered to the bouncer, who let her through with no problem. Before Kanika could say another word, Tiffany and Shanae turned and got lost in the pulsating lights of the club.

Kanika and Peaches nearly broke their necks turning around glancing at the fine, tall brothers looking clean in their linens, jean outfits, and leathers and furs even though it was summer. Every eye seemed to stay glued on Kanika, like she had "new bitch in town" stamped on her forehead.

"Two Malibu pineapples please," Peaches said as they walked up to the busy bar. Peaches smiled flirtatiously at a guy dressed in a red and white suit.

"That is just your style, girl. Them ole-school men. What is he thinking?" Kanika asked.

"What is he driving is more like it. Those older cats not only got bank but pension plans, real estate. Don't sleep." As usual, Kanika paid for their drinks and surveyed the club for a cool spot to chill. "Tyrell counts as an older man, you know."

"Where did that come from?" Kanika said, glancing at Peaches from the corner of her eye.

"He's almost seven years older than you. He would qualify in my book." Peaches laughed.

"Uhm, he is qualified all around. That age shit don't mean nothing," Kanika said, studying who the hustlers were. They were the ugliest guys with the prettiest women and the longest pockets. She caught a few checking her out. Gold strappy heels complemented her look with gold bangles and earrings. Though it was dressy for New York club standards, at Ambiance it seemed like the norm. Some of the women even had promlike dresses on, and the infamous multicolored cropped fur jackets even though it was summer.

All the girls sat around the VIP area in the lounge. Kanika was used to partying in style and not standing around with the common folks. Kanika ordered six bottles of Dom P. and a platter of jumbo cocktail shrimp. The clout and the name her family made for themselves made it easy for Kanika to buy the damn bar with no ID, if she wanted to. Everyone thanked her but Tiffany.

"This champagne is good as hell!" Shanae said, smacking her lips. "I can't remember the last time I had me some Dom. What about you, Tiff?"

"I had some with breakfast this morning," Tiffany said, wolfing down her fourth glass.

Kanika rolled her eyes.

Once the club filled to capacity and everyone was

on the floor, Kanika and Peaches decided to make their rounds. Kanika wasn't looking for anything in particular, but it was a good time to help her forget what she was missing.

"Oh no, this is our song, Kanika!" Peaches shouted as they both began to dance to Lil' Kim's "Get Money."

It was just like being back home, Kanika thought, as she tried her best to get in the groove while sipping her Malibu pineapple. Within no time, the guy in the red and white suit was behind Peaches, getting his grind on.

An overweight brother, short, with an unruly 'fro, wearing a gray silk suit and about six gold chains around his neck, walked up to Kanika. *Look at his countrified ass,* she thought.

"Whatsup, Ms. Sexy Thang?" the brother said, licking his lips as he practically drooled over her juicy thighs.

"Whatsup?" Kanika said, covering her nose. His breath was ferocious and she politely backed away. Just then she noticed Tiffany watching her like a hawk from the other side of the room. Shanae was still seated in VIP, nursing a bottle of Dom P. with a cutie.

Two samurai-size brothers pulled Tiffany onto the dance floor and sandwiched her between them. Tiffany started grinding on both of them. Kanika realized she was the only one not having a good time. An old LL song, "Jingling Baby," rang through the speakers, and Kanika could not stand still any longer. She immersed herself in the tempestuous rhythm. The song made her feel sexy and proud of that big wagon she was dragging. In no time, she had a man's hard body against her. He was about five-eleven, a gray linen shirt covering his sturdy build.

She turned around and wiggled her behind against him and sipped her drink. Her mind felt free and her body loose as the bass and tempo of the song picked up. The whole club was singing along, "Go 'head, baby, they're jingling, baby, go 'head, baby . . ."

"I'm jingling, baby!" Kanika said, silently thanking the liquor for helping her unwind.

"Don't hurt me now," said her dance partner, smiling down at her and into her bouncing breasts.

Kanika smiled back and just kept doing her thing. She didn't want to know his name or need his number. It was all about her, in her own little world.

"I'm Jason," he bent down and said in her ear as the song switched to "Paid in Full," a Rakim classic.

"Hi," Kanika said, unamused. When she looked over, she caught Shanae staring at her big eyed, with her mouth wide open. She made an "OK" sign to Kanika.

"Seems like your friends approve of me," Jason said, holding on to Kanika's swaying hips.

"They don't count. It's what I think."

"Let me get your number."

"I got a man already."

"I'm Jason, Jay Love. Every chick out here wants

me, boo. You must be new," he said, sporting a grin
and pulling her toward his chest.

Asshole, Kanika thought. "Excuse me, but I gotta
go to the ladies' room," she said, snatching her arm
back.

She wasn't even completely off the dance floor
when Shanae and Tiffany blocked her way.

"What's up with y'all?" Kanika said, baffled by
their disbelieving looks.

"Honey, that's Jay Love. He's like *da man* around
here. He got like five cars, and run a lot of shit down
in North Carolina. He know Daddy," Tiffany said.

"Well, that's good and all, but he's not my type,"
Kanika answered, walking around them and heading
toward Peaches. Tiffany and Shanae followed her.

"What's going on, y'all? I got me three numbers.
One cat is from New York," Peaches said.

"Good for you," Tiffany said drily.

"Kanika, you are trippin about Jay Love." Shanae
laughed and held up her drink. "You a real diva, cutting motherfuckas off at the knees! Jay Love don't
step to no girls. Ain't that right, Tiff?"

Tiffany's light-skinned face turned beet red, and
her lip curled in distaste. "What the fuck? Kanika
don't even know what she was doing. That nigga
probably stepped to her because of her fat ass."

"Well, at least he stepped to her. When was the last
time you pulled a nigga like Jay Love?" Shanae said,
tapping one foot as she waited for Tiffany's answer.

Kanika felt embarrassed. She could care less

about Jay Love. She didn't want Tiffany to take it too seriously, in case she did like him.

"Please, I don't want his country ass," Kanika said, rolling her eyes. She looked at Tiffany and smiled, but Tiffany shot her a look filled with venom.

For the rest of the evening, Kanika hung out with Shanae and Peaches. Tiffany had a funky attitude and didn't talk to any of them for the rest of the evening. *Whatever,* Kanika thought. She didn't have time for Tiffany's stank ass, anyway.

Back at the house, Tiffany ignored Kanika, but Kanika didn't sweat it. She had bigger fish to fry with her man, instead of worrying about someone else's. When she reached her bedroom, she saw that Tyrell had called three times between 12:00 and 2:00 A.M. She must have had her phone on vibrate. She held her breath as she dialed his number.

"Hello?" a deep, throaty voice said on the first ring.

"Hey, boo, it's me. I went out with Peaches," Kanika said, as if she was confessing. "She was down here checking me out, but she's driving back up to New York in the morning."

"So what she talkin' about?" he said, sarcastically.

Kanika's rolled her eyes. "Nothing, we just had fun. I need some fun. I thought about you the whole time."

He paused and then he laughed lightly. "I'm sorry about what happened last night."

"I know you under a lot of stress. But try to understand, so am I."

"It's all gonna get better from here. I promise you."

Kanika paused. "My daddy says he wants to help find Mommy's killer."

"I got all that on lock," Tyrell said angrily. "I'm doing all I can."

"I know, but I was just sayin'."

"Baby, trust me. You gotta trust me."

Kanika swallowed her grief. "I trust you with all I got."

"I'm almost finished cleaning up some business around here. I got the police off my back; I got Tony's—I mean my, suppliers happy again, money coming in. I'll be down soon."

"The police?"

"Well, you know how they like sweating a brother," he said, his voice turning low.

"Oh."

"So what you wearing?" he asked, his tone soft and buried in some kind of kinky fantasy.

"Nothing—" Kanika slipped under the covers and turned her night lamp off.

Fifteen

Kanika had been in Virginia for a little over a month. Just two weeks into college, she was knee-deep in papers, studying, and just trying to stay ahead. This wasn't what she was used to. She'd always mastered her classes, especially math, and her grades were always top-notch. But for now, school helped make the days go by faster and easier.

"How school going? They got you dissecting frogs and shit yet?" Shon grinned as he opened a can of sardines in the kitchen.

"That's high school biology. I'm studying economics." Kanika rubbed her tired eyes as she strained to read her textbook.

"I know, I know, just asking. I really like how you take your schoolwork seriously. I think if your mother had stayed in school she'd be leading some big company now," he said, sounding like he missed her.

"Really?" Kanika knew that could be true, but she wanted to urge him on and see what else her daddy had to say about her mother.

"She was just like you are now. Always good with numbers. She'd help me count my G-stacks, host my parties, and even did my motherfuckin' taxes." He laughed. "She knew how to take care of her man."

Kanika slowly closed her textbook. "What else did you like about Mommy so much?"

Her father sat on the other side of the kitchen island with a smug look. "I think your ears too young to hear that part!"

"Tell me."

His gaze focused on Kanika's face as if he was recalling a very private moment he had had with Waleema. "You know them sandwich wetters your mama got? Well, let's just say she put them to good use on a nigga," he said, shaking his head.

Kanika shuddered. She had no desire to hear about her parents' sex life. "But what else?"

"I'm just getting started. Waleema had power and she knew how to use it. She had me kissing her feet one moment and ready to backslap her ass the next. I was going in circles with that woman." Kanika was pleasantly surprised at her father's openness. Maybe he was starting to trust her, she thought.

"So why did you treat her so bad?"

He studied her for several long moments. She thought he wasn't going to answer when he said, "I knew she was smarter than me, and the only upper had I had was my backhand and gutter mouth. One thing I can do is cuss a bitch out."

Kanika tried not to reveal how her father's confession had affected her. Suddenly she saw him in a different way. He seemed human, not cold and icy. But then again, this was her daddy, and he was a great manipulator.

"I don't know what your mama told you, but she left me. Sure I was fucking with her mind, trying to keep her for myself one day and let her know she can be out the door the next. But I never really wanted her to go."

"Why didn't you stop her?"

He laughed, popping a sardine in his mouth. A few drops of oil missed his wrinkle-free Sean John jeans and Armani button-down shirt. "Your mama is like hell on wheels when she gets ready to make a move. I got out of her way." Shon cleaned the meat off the sardine and slid the bone out between his teeth.

Kanika opened up her textbook again. "I heard a different story, and it wasn't easy for Mommy and me. But we made it."

Shon ate two more sardines as he watched her get back into her books. Then he said, "You remind me so much of her. The way you look, the way you shaped. Do you know how beautiful you are?"

Kanika fidgeted in her seat at her father's tone, but didn't answer.

He sucked the fish grease from his fingers. "I bet you make your man real happy. Don't you?"

Kanika slowly looked up and watched him pick his teeth. He was only in his thirties and looked like he was in his twenties. "Tyrell is very happy. Mommy really liked him, too."

"Anyway." Her father waved his hand like he was swatting a fly. "You wanna make your daddy real happy?"

Kanika grabbed some red grapes from the bowl on the counter. "Um, what do you need?" She knew her father was up to something.

"I like your style. You and Tiffany are the same age, almost, but you way more mature than her. How would you like to meet some important people?"

Kanika put her elbows on the table and leaned in closer. She was always up for making a new connection. "What you got in mind?"

"I want you to host my next party. It'll be at a plantation I reserved on the white side of town. Next weekend."

Kanika smiled. "I'd love to. Is Tiffany hosting, too?"

"Nah." He sneered. "She don't have the class for that. Don't tell her you hosting, either. I'll tell her."

"Can Tyrell come?"

"Who?"

"Tyrell. My man."

"Kanika, there are gonna be some top-dog niggas in there. Why would you bring sand to the beach?" He sported a devilish smile.

"Well, I don't mind hosting, but I'm not interested in anyone else right now."

"Hm," Shon said, studying her once again. "So tell me about this nigga Tyrell. Why you so hung up on him? If it wasn't for him—"

"Uh-uh, Daddy, don't do that!" Kanika said, sticking a finger in the air. "Tyrell did what he could. This was a straight-up ambush. He's doing what he can now to keep at least Tony's name alive."

"So he taking Tony's spot. Now he gonna get bank off of that nigga's hard work. That shit don't sound crazy to you?"

"Please, he worked alongside Tony. That money is his, too. You sounding crazy now," Kanika said, looking him up and down.

He smiled. "Did Tyrell and Tony get along?"

"He was Tony's right hand," Kanika said immediately. But she remembered some of Tyrell's frustrations with Tony's style of business.

Kanika's father brought the empty can of sardines to his mouth and sipped the juice. "From what I understand, ain't nobody like that mothafucka Tony but your mama."

"He was good to us. So I don't give a damn who has something to say, including *you*."

Her father laughed. "I love that attitude about you, baby," he said, walking up to her. He leaned down and kissed her cheek. "So smart, but so young."

"Tyrell protected all of us, Daddy. He sent me

down here to be safe," she said, feeling cold. She rubbed her arms to warm herself.

"So why he the only one breathing, while your mama and Tony is dead?" Her father strolled out of the kitchen. Kanika felt the frigidness he left behind.

Sixteen

On Friday night, Peaches was back in town. She was making regular visits to Virginia now. It wasn't so much that she liked the Virginia charm, but her girl was down there. Though Peaches and her man were all good, she was never one to turn down another brother who was caked up. Any time she hung with Kanika the fellas would flock around her like bees to honey, and Peaches wanted to be around to catch the strays.

This time, the hot spot was The Cottage, the quintessential D.C. spot that welcomed celebrities from every sector of music and sports. Kanika had Peaches flown in just to hang out. Right after Peaches' arrival, Tiffany persuaded Kanika to take the two-hour drive to The Cottage's big Labor Day party. Kanika wasn't so sure about traveling out of state, especially in a flashy rented powder blue Benz coupe. She preferred to fly or take the first-class car in the express train, where she could lounge and be served. But the two-hour drive went by faster than she expected.

As the others posed in the VIP area, Kanika wrote Tyrell a text message. She had told him her plans earlier but just wanted him to feel her wherever he was. By the time Kanika placed an order for several bottles of Grey Goose and Cristal for herself and her girls, Tyrell sent her a sexy text message back reading: *I may be up there soon. It's a surprise. Just get that pussy ready.*

Kanika smiled and read the message at least four times. *It's about time that Negro got his ass down here,* she said to herself. She was tired of hearing "soon." She wanted dates. But he wanted it to be a surprise. She thought that was so romantic of him.

"Girl, is you gonna sit there and stare at that damn cell phone all night? There is too much money and too little time up in this piece," Peaches said, holding her flute up to the waitress for more Dom P.

"I was just checking something," Kanika said, slipping the phone back into her tiny leopard-print purse. "I think Tyrell may be coming to see me soon."

"Exactly! That is why you need to shake that ass tonight and get you some numbers," Peaches said, pointing across the room. "Who knows when that nigga is really coming?"

"Uh, no, Peaches, don't fuck about Tyrell like that. He got a lotta shit on his mind right now," Kanika said, waving her hand.

"That's why you don't need to be all up in his ass. Just chill tonight and get you something. At least a free drink for you and your girl," she said, flashing a mean grin.

Then Shanae blurted out, "Yes, y'all, and I am checking something out, right here and now!" She was looking at the room below, where folks were dancing and girls dressed in bras and panties were swinging from long iron poles.

"Who, what, what?" Tiffany said, jumping up. "Is that Shaquille?"

"No, fool." Shanae laughed. "Somebody just as paid, but much cuter."

"Let me see," Tiffany said, pushing them out of the way. All the girls, except Kanika, ran to the railing for a better view. By their animated conversation Kanika knew something serious was going on. She wondered if it was Puffy or anybody.

"Who is it?" Kanika said, not able to hold back her own curiosity. She walked up to the rail.

"Chile, that's Saliq! My soon-to-be baby daddy," Shanae said, shaking Kanika's shoulders.

"I'd like to take a long sip of his bathwater." Peaches laughed. Kanika hissed under her breath at Peaches. She hated the way Peaches was so desperate for any kind of male attention. To her, it was pathetic, but men ate it up.

Saliq was standing at the edge of the bar towering over all the others around him, looking cool and undisturbed by all the activity.

"Shanae, Kanika don't know what time it is. Let me go say hi to that fool." Tiffany pulled out a small mirror and smeared an extra coat of cherry lip gloss on her already-glossy lips. "The fellas like the lips big and shiny," she said, adjusting the cleavage in her low-cut blouse, and glided down the steps and walked in Saliq's direction.

"Why is Tiffany acting so stupid over him?" Peaches asked Shanae.

"Honey, he bought his last girlfriend a Jaguar for her birthday and he only knew her for two months." Shanae and Peaches kept their eyes sealed on Tiffany working her way to Saliq.

Kanika casually walked back to the VIP table to pour herself a glass of champagne.

"Come here! Look at this," Shanae said, motioning for Kanika to spy with them.

Like three owls on a branch, they all watched Tiffany work her hips as she approached Saliq. Finally the crowd parted or Saliq turned around; Kanika couldn't remember which happened first. But her heart did a pitter-patter when she saw him. Saliq looked like an NFL linebacker, with a wide, thick body and broad shoulders. He was dressed in jeans and a black button-down shirt. He looked laid-back and not flashy at all to be one of the "most paid niggas" in Virginia. He was surrounded mostly by women vying for his attention.

"Oh no," Shanae sighed. "You see that look he is giving Tiff? What is up with her neck motions?"

Shanae and Peaches cracked up laughing. Kanika just watched as Tiffany tried hard to get some conversation out of him, but he just nodded to the music and ignored anything Tiffany was saying. Tiffany was obviously getting heated when she turned around and saw them watching. She threw up her hand as if to tell them to stop gawking at her.

Shanae and Peaches giggled like two schoolgirls. "She should let me handle that. I know how to talk to a man. She is running her mouth too damn much," Peaches said.

Kanika just shook her head and signaled for Tiffany to come back. Just then Saliq looked up and caught Kanika's eye. She felt her breath catch. It was that same look he gave her in the rearview mirror that day on the trip from the airport. Then he leaned down and whispered something in Tiffany's ear.

"Oh my God, he finally said something to her," Shanae said, with her hand over her mouth. "We probably put him on the spot. He better be buying us all drinks."

Kanika saw that Tiffany was no longer smiling. She looked up at them and waved them all down. Peaches almost tripped over Shanae trying to be the first one down the steps. Kanika came, too, not at all eager like the others. The feelings Saliq evoked in her made her wary.

After stepping on what felt like three hundred pairs of toes, Kanika and the other girls finally reached

Tiffany, who was standing there looking frustrated with her arms folded.

"Hello, ladies," Saliq said, nodding his head to everyone but keeping his eye on Kanika. Kanika shifted uncomfortably. He was a handsome brother with his caramel skin, deep-set bedroom eyes, and chiseled jaw. Even though the club smelled like smoke, she still caught a whiff of his Cool Water cologne. He leaned against the bar, looking strong, relaxed, and confident.

"This is my friend Shanae and this is Peaches," Tiffany said, introducing everyone but Kanika to Saliq.

Peaches threw Tiffany a nasty look and stood shoulder-to-shoulder with Kanika.

"How y'all doing?" he said, his voice as deep and smooth as her mama's satin sheets. "Hey, Kanika. I was wondering when I was gonna see you again."

Kanika stepped around and held her hand out for Saliq to shake. "Nice to see you again. I'm at Hampton now until I go back to New York." She could feel Tiffany's glare.

"Not if I have anything to do with that." Saliq smiled and kissed her hand.

"Yeah, she like our little ghetto princess from up north," Shanae said, throwing her arm around Kanika's shoulders.

"Now can we get some drinks?" Peaches said, her arms folded against her chest.

"What is your problem?" Kanika whispered in Peaches' ear. "You don't have to ask."

"You can at least get him to do that, because I know you about to be up under that nigga all night," Peaches said, her eyes almost looking watery with anger.

"Isn't that what you said I should be doing? You are really tripping tonight." Kanika laughed but felt sorry for her, too. Peaches must be tired of being overlooked, she thought. But the fact that she wasn't blessed with what it takes wasn't Kanika's fault, either.

Saliq signaled to one of his boys to bring the ladies a round of whatever they wanted.

"No, I'm still working on this champagne," Kanika said, feeling unusually nervous about him. She turned to Peaches to try to get her to talk to one of Saliq's boys, but she was already on the case.

"Wanna dance?" Saliq asked as a slow Jodeci classic, "Forever My Lady," filled the club.

He didn't give her a chance to respond, which was just as well since words escaped her. His tall, thick body wrapped around hers, sheltered her like home, a place that, lately, she had only visited in her dreams. She closed her eyes without even realizing it. It felt good to be in a man's arms again.

After The Cottage, Peaches went home with Kanika. Her aunt Icelene lived too far, another hour's drive, to go there that night.

Kanika saw her father in the kitchen eating half a turkey sandwich. He hadn't met Peaches, and Kanika thought it was rude to have a friend up in the house without letting her father know. And he was around, which was a rare thing, too.

"Daddy, this is my friend Peaches, from New York. She's here for the weekend," Kanika said, dragging Peaches into the kitchen. They both were dead tired, and all Kanika wanted to do was sleep.

But as soon as Peaches set eyes on Shon, she was at full attention. "Hello, Mr. Jones. It's so nice to finally meet Kanika's father."

Shon wiped his hands and shook Peaches' hand. "Nice to meet you. What you two ladies been up to?" he asked, not even seeming to mind that Kanika was bringing folks up in the house. Her father might be cool after all, Kanika thought.

"We just came from the club. We're ready to go to bed," Kanika said, nodding to Peaches.

"Yeah, Mr. Jones, we had a lot of fun. Maybe you can come sometimes?" Peaches asked, smiling wide at her father.

Kanika had to look at her twice. *Oh, no, she isn't!* she thought.

"I got my own spots. Grown and sexy spots," he said, smiling.

Kanika was cutting this flirtation off at the knees. She grabbed Peaches' arm.

"Good night," she said and she and Peaches walked out of the kitchen.

"Oh, Mr. Jones, you still have some mayonnaise on your top lip," Peaches pointed out.

Shon wiped it away and nodded a thank-you, as the girls walked up the steps. Kanika didn't remember seeing anything on her father's mouth.

Just before they went to bed, Peaches asked, "So how did it feel dancing with Saliq?" as she lay on the blue and white daybed across from Kanika. "You guys were holding each other kind of close."

"*He* was holding *me*," Kanika said. She slipped on a pair of yellow-gold silk pajama pants and top and tossed Peaches a similar pajama set. "But why do I feel guilty?"

"Because you like him?" Peaches nestled herself in the cozy, soft daybed and covered her feet with the cool cotton sheet.

"Do I?" Kanika asked. "I mean, it was just a dance, but I can't deny how fine he is. He looks like Tyrell, too."

Peaches stared at Kanika.

"Don't you think he does?" Kanika asked her as she turned off the lights. "I know Tiffany must be so jealous now."

Peaches said nothing.

"Girl, you ain't 'sleep yet, are you?"

"I think I should tell you something."

Kanika rolled over on her side. It was too dark to see Peaches' face. "What?"

Peaches huffed, "I been wanting to talk to you all

night, but you looked like you was having so much fun." Her tone was sarcastic.

"Just come out with it."

"I don't know about this for sure, but just a few days ago I saw Tyrell driving by my house. He wasn't alone."

"OK," Kanika said slowly, waiting for more. Her heart started to pound.

"There was some dark-skinned chick I have never seen before around the way in the passenger seat. I mean, I never got a good look at her because he was driving. She kind of looked like you, except for your Asian eyes."

Kanika flew off the bed. She flipped back on the lights. "Where the fuck is my phone!" she said, tearing around the room for her Chanel purse. She found her bag, dug out her cell phone, and started to dial. "Let's see what that nigga got to say."

"Wait; wait, girl!" Peaches said, getting up off the bed. "It could be anyone."

"Ain't no need for guessing games," Kanika said.

Peaches sat beside her on the edge of the bed and watched Kanika as she waited for him to pick up.

"Hello?"

"So who sucking your dick?" Kanika asked, her hands trembling with anger. Her body felt hot like she had a fever.

"Nika?" Tyrell asked.

"Yes, nigga! Peaches just told me she seen you

with some dark-skinned trick. Tyrell, don't fucking lie to me!"

"Are you and Peaches high on some shit?"

"Answer me!"

"That bitch is a liar! Stank ho!" he said, knowing that Peaches was on a mission to break them up and he fell right into her hands.

Kanika looked at Peaches, then at the phone. "She is my best friend, Tyrell."

"That bitch is evil. You gonna choose her over me?"

Kanika looked at Peaches, who was biting her nails down. She felt helpless. She was miles away from her man. She didn't want to be selfish, but last night showed her, even she needed male companionship. She took a deep breath.

"Look, I know things are hard for us now. But just promise you'll always be loyal to me."

"I can promise you my loyalty, baby. Forever."

Kanika hung up.

"So what he say?"

"He is loyal to me and I'm loyal to him. That's all we need."

She missed the look in Peaches' eyes.

Seventeen

The following morning, Kanika woke up alone in her bedroom. It was 9:00 A.M. and she could clock more hours in bed, but she hoped she and Peaches would be able to get a head start on some shopping before Peaches left to return to New York.

"Peaches?" Kanika asked, knocking on the bathroom door. The tiles in the shower were still beaded with water from Peaches' shower. Kanika grabbed her black silk robe, slipped into it, and tied the belt around her waist. When she checked her cell phone, she saw that Saliq had called a few hours ago.

She walked down to Tiffany's room, peeked through the door, and found Tiffany snoring. Kanika heard the clinking of dishes, then the sounds of laughter coming from the kitchen, so she walked downstairs.

"Daddy?" Kanika asked, standing at the doorway of the kitchen. There were her father and Peaches having waffles, bacon, and freshly squeezed orange juice.

"Hey, baby," her father said, smiling. He had on a gray silk bathrobe over his silk pajamas. "Peaches made us all breakfast."

"Oh," Kanika said, not feeling as cheerful as Peaches and her dad looked.

"Come on, girl, sit down with us. There's plenty."

Kanika saw only three slices of bacon and a lone waffle left. It looked like Peaches had made this breakfast for two. Peaches still had on the pajama set that Kanika had lent her, but now the open belly portion seemed like too much skin to be showing off in front of Shon. Kanika sat down and just observed Peaches and her father. Her antenna was up.

"Peaches, you wanna go shopping later? I know you gotta leave soon," Kanika said, hoping to get some alone time together with Peaches before she left.

Shon looked at Peaches. Then at Kanika.

"I asked Peaches to stay with us. It's the summer and you may need a real friend around." Her father winked at her.

Kanika stared at her father. He was up to something. Even Peaches looked surprised.

"Peaches, what about your job and your moms?" Kanika asked.

"I'll tell her, I guess. Thank you, Mr. Jones. We can spend more time together now, Kanika," Peaches said, laughing.

"I invited Peaches to the party, too."

Kanika's eyes went from Peaches to her father again. He was flirting with Peaches, smiling and setting eyes on her every now and again.

"I'm going back upstairs," Kanika said. She couldn't watch any more of this. "Are we still going shopping?" she asked Peaches.

"Well, um, I'm going back to New York for the weekend to get some things. I'm leaving this afternoon, but I'll be back Monday night."

"I wish I could go with you," Kanika said under her breath.

"The hell you are!" her father shouted.

Again Peaches and her father looked at each other.

"Whatever. I'll catch up with you later. Since you are gonna be living here," Kanika added in a mocking way.

Kanika marched back up the steps. She wasn't angry at Peaches but felt like her friend was being slick. Kanika paused at the top of the steps and listened. She heard more laughs, mostly from Peaches, then quietness. Kanika crept back down the steps and toward the kitchen. She had to blink several times to make sure she wasn't seeing things.

Her father's pajamas were gathered at his ankles. Peaches' lips were glued to his black dick sucking on it like it was a lollipop. Kanika wanted to run in there and smack the shit out of both of them. She knew that Peaches had sucked off more than she could handle.

◆ ◆ ◆

When Kanika returned from Hampton Roads, she was empty-handed. Her mind had been too busy to concentrate on shopping, which was a first. She spent most of the time in her car, watching other shoppers, and sitting at a nearby café. She needed to prep herself to see Peaches again. She shook her head. *That bitch is just a straight-up ho.* When she got home she was going to put everybody in their place.

But when she got there she was in for a big surprise. Her bed was covered with a colorful assortment of designer dresses, pants, gowns, and suits made of the softest, most luxurious fabrics.

"What is this?" she said, running her hands across the clothes. She held a plum-colored Prada silk dress up to her body and modeled it in the mirror. She twirled around and did the same for the Versace and Oscar de la Renta dresses. Someone knocked at her door.

"Daddy, did you do this?" Kanika said, holding up a vintage pink Chanel suit.

"I want you to look like a princess when you host the party next weekend. Not that you aren't already," he said. "Pick out whatever you want to wear, and keep the rest. Thank Tiffany, too; she went to Saks and helped."

Kanika wondered how many pussy licks it took this time. She shook her head and shook the idea right out. "Daddy, um, what the hell is going on with you and Peaches?"

"Come on now; I'm a grown man," he said, shrugging her off.

"I know, but I saw her sucking your dick. That's my friend. We're the same age."

"Let's just say Peaches acts a little older." He laughed.

"Are you fucking Peaches?"

"Man, listen, you are not my woman," Shon said, his finger almost touching the tip of Kanika's nose.

"Is this your way of testing my loyalty or something, because that is sick!" Kanika said, shaking her head.

"I do what I please and fuck who I please in *my* house. Get that right. *My* house! And as long as you in *my* house, you stay out of my motherfuckin' business." He still held his finger in Kanika's face.

She turned her face away. "Get the fuck away from me." She wasn't letting any man put his hands on or near her, not even her so-called father. Kanika realized this was not a conversation to have with him. She couldn't wait to get into Peaches' ass about all this.

"And you better not try to get your little attitude with Peaches, either, when she gets back. Because she'll tell me."

"What?" Kanika cocked her neck to the side like he was speaking a foreign language.

"And you better not have any big ideas about fucking up my party," he said, with an icy grill. "I don't care what your mama did, but I will beat ya ass."

Kanika wasn't going to test that one.

Eighteen

On her way home from class on Monday afternoon, Kanika fought to stay awake at the wheel. She was only a few minutes from the house, but the night before she had gotten only three hours of sleep. There was just too much partying and daydreaming about Tyrell, which had her motivation for school all off. Not exactly the best way to prepare for her first college exam, she thought. She didn't even want to think about the grade she was going to get on the math test she had taken this morning. Even though it was her favorite subject, she always brushed up before a test—always. And she was also two days late to turn in an analytical essay for her supply and demand course.

When Kanika got inside the house, she dragged herself up the long spiral staircase and into her bed. Her first instinct was to call Tyrell, she needed someone to talk to about Peaches, but she had too much on her plate. She grabbed her laptop and pressed the "on" button.

Her cell phone rang loud enough that it made her jump up. Her nerves were shot, too, she thought, rubbing her head.

"Hello?" she said.

"Whatsup? You OK?" Tyrell asked, with a slew of sirens and music in the background.

"I'm fine. Where you at?"

"I'm outside the barbershop waiting to get my hair cut. You sound tired."

"I got to class late, and need to finish a paper." Kanika set her laptop on her lap. "I may have too much on my mind."

"You wanna talk about it?"

"Do you know that Peaches is staying with us now?" she said.

Tyrell made a sound. "What do you mean? . . . I mean how is she stayin' with you?" he asked carefully.

"She's fucking Daddy, that's how," Kanika said, anger flowing through her.

"I told you that bitch is a true ass ho," Tyrell said.

"My daddy probably caused all this."

"That's some foul shit right there."

"My father is such a fucking pig."

"I ain't one to throw salt in another man's game. I know how that is. But she's supposed to be your girl. I would kick it to her and be like, 'What really good?' "

"Since I been here, he and I haven't even had no

time together like they have." Kanika stopped. She was jealous.

"So what you and your pops be doing?"

"Talking and shit. He wants me to host one of his baller parties next weekend. Like my mommy used to," she told him.

"You doing that?"

"Yeah. It's something my mother was good at. And eventually I'ma have to do it for you, too," she said.

"Uhm, you know my shit is more low-key than that. Why you agree to do that?"

"I just told you, Tyrell. Plus, it gives me something to do. It's not like you down here trying to see me."

"Yeah, aight," he said, after a long pause.

Kanika opened her eyes wide and said, "You know, I was thinking maybe I can come see you. Just for a day or two."

There was a pause, then Tyrell said, "Nah, I'm coming down there this weekend."

Kanika didn't want to invite him to the party because her father made it clear he didn't want Tyrell there, plus Saliq was going to be there. She didn't want Saliq and Tyrell getting into any shit.

He grunted. "I'm over here losing it without seeing you."

"Losing it how?"

"I just need to see you soon."

"Is Mommy's house and the plants okay?"

"Everything is taken care of. The plants are still looking good. I just want you up here for good," he said, greeting someone, though Kanika couldn't hear who.

"Hello?"

"Watch your daddy's friends. If they anything like him, they gonna want some of that young pussy."

"I can take care of myself, Tyrell." Kanika smiled.

"I love you," he said in a suddenly solemn tone. "I don't want to lose you."

"Same here, boo," she said, thinking he sounded real down. "I love you, too."

"One," he said, and hung up.

Kanika put her cell phone down and felt an immense sense of guilt. She hadn't even thought about another guy until she met Saliq. She planned to let Saliq know she was happy with Tyrell and let him down easy at the party.

Kanika took a cool, refreshing shower before she went to bed around midnight. When she got out, she found Peaches sitting on her bed, waiting for her. Though Peaches felt foul for seeing Kanika's dad, like everything in their relationship, Kanika's approval meant everything.

Peaches' hair was in rollers and her eyes were bloodshot. She looked like she had been pushed out of bed. Before Kanika could protest at her presence, Peaches blurted, "Don't be tripping about me and your daddy, girl. I'm sure he been fucking women half his age. And I'm legal."

Kanika sucked her teeth at her and looked at

Peaches. "My father is thirty-eight, and you are eighteen. I would not give a fuck if he was some dude from the street. I'd be like 'go get yours.' But that's my daddy. And if he do anything to hurt you, that can destroy our friendship," she said.

Peaches wiped her eyes with a tissue. "I know, and that's the last thing I want. But I don't want you to think for a minute that he made me do anything. When I saw that picture of your father when I first came to see you, I thought he was fine. He looked so young. And basically, I just wanted to fuck him. It was me, Kanika, not him."

"So you did have sex?" Kanika said, one hand on her hip.

Peaches took a long, deep inhalation. "That morning when we came back from the club. I heard your father walking around. I went downstairs and we started talking. Then I made breakfast."

"And then you started *fucking*," Kanika said, shaking her head. "Spare me any more details," Kanika said, sitting beside Peaches on the daybed.

Peaches rubbed Kanika's shoulders. "I want my best friend back. I don't want this to get between us. It was my mistake. I'm sorry."

Kanika held her head down. "Is that all you came in here to say? Are you sleeping in his bed tonight, too?"

Peaches wavered with her answer, then said, "He gives me money, Kanika. Maybe I can finally afford the things you have."

Kanika was finally beginning to put the pieces together. She spotted Peaches' new diamond bracelet and her sad eyes. Peaches wasn't broke, but she didn't have a fat trust fund and other things that came with Kanika's lifestyle. "Everything I have, my moms gave to me. And it got blood all over it. One who lives by the sword dies by the sword. You don't want this life."

"You get to host fancy parties—" Peaches said, her round face looking childlike.

"But you got your moms; I don't. I don't even have a real father," she said, referring to Shon. "All I have is Tyrell."

"Nika, your father loves you to death. All he talks about is how you smart you are, how you look like your mother, how he wants to keep you in VA." Peaches curled into a fetal position in the bed and wrapped the bedspread around her.

"Well, that last part ain't happening." Kanika got up, slipped off her robe, and put on a freshly washed peach silk nightgown.

She turned off the lights. She noticed Peaches didn't leave.

"Still deciding where to sleep tonight?" Kanika said mockingly. She was still angry. She didn't know if she could go back to being best friends with Peaches, like they were.

Nineteen

Kanika met her father at Oscar's, a high-end seafood restaurant near Virginia Beach. It had beautiful tall white columns on the inside and palm trees on the outside. There was an unbelievable ocean view of the Atlantic and the fresh, crisp smell of the sea breeze. He had arranged for them to have a talk. Kanika thought Peaches had something to do with this, and she was looking forward to it. There were a few things she needed to get off her chest, too.

A chilled bottle of Moët sat in an ice bucket when she arrived.

"I'm glad you didn't stand me up," Shon said in a gentle way. He gave her a kiss on the cheek. Kanika wiped her face and sat.

"I hope that's not about Peaches," he said, looking suave in a gold-striped white shirt and gold-colored pants.

She broke a piece of bread in half. She unfolded a

white napkin over her lap, making sure not to soil her brand-new Iceberg jean shorts outfit. "I'm trying to get used to it."

"Sorry about the other night. I didn't mean to yell at you like that. But I *did* mean everything I said." His eyes twinkled with intensity. *"Everything."*

Kanika looked around uncomfortably and saw a couple of professional-looking black women checking out her daddy. They were seated by a water fountain.

"Did you hear what I said?"

She slipped on a pair of Gucci shades at the table. "Yes, Daddy, I heard you. So why are we meeting like this then?"

A slender Hispanic waiter came along and laid down a platter of baked clams, Italian style, and shrimp cocktails. Those were two of Kanika's favorites. She picked a few clams and placed them on her plate.

"I'm leaving for New York, after the party this weekend. I told you I was gonna find out who killed your mama," Shon said, pulling a shrimp out of its shell with his teeth. "And that's what I'm gonna do."

Strands of Kanika's wavy hair whipped her in the face from the breeze. She knew that was bullshit. Her father had people to do that kind of legwork for him. He was hiding something. "Can I come?"

"Hell, no," he said, elegantly sipping his champagne. "Too dangerous for you, but I got some of my old connects up there. They can fill me in on what's really happening."

"I told you, Tyrell is handling that."

"I like to get my info from my own sources."

Kanika stared at the bubbles in her champagne. She was through trying to challenge her father. And she didn't want her mood too messed up before Tyrell arrived. "Is Peaches going with you?"

"Peaches is staying," he said. "In my bedroom."

Kanika shook her head in dismay and swallowed a clam. "Great."

"So you ready for the party this weekend? That shit is gonna be off the chain," Shon said, blowing a kiss to one of the women who kept watching him. "Which dress you wearing? Anything would look good on that body."

"I haven't decided what to wear yet. I'm gonna be busy with some stuff at the school for a few days. I may even spend the night there," she said.

"At school?" her father asked, taking a clam.

"Yeah. This girl I'm working on this economics paper with lives in the dorm. And we got mad work to do. It's a team project," she said, her gold bangles jingling as she called the waiter over.

"Oh," her father said, suspiciously eyeing her.

"More clams, please," she told the waiter and blew her father a fake kiss. Tyrell may not have been invited to the party, but Virginia was a big place.

Twenty

Thursday night, Kanika was knocking on Tyrell's door at the Marriott. He had sent her an instant message with his room number about an hour ago. He opened the door wrapped in a white towel from his waist down.

Kanika said nothing, and neither did Tyrell, both eager to just touch. She wrapped her legs and arms around him. They stumbled inside the room, and fell onto the floor. Peeling out of her clothes, Kanika pinned Tyrell to the ground with her arms and lips. They sucked on each other's tongues like they were lollipops; their hands wandered to each other's familiar parts. Kanika walked her fingers down his well-built chest and his body down to his loose dick. She smiled as she caressed his throbbing dick with her long, manicured fingernails. Tyrell sat up on his elbows while she sucked and licked him from the tip of his head to his balls, deep-throating him until she couldn't take in any more. She picked up some remnants of Irish Spring soap and lost her nose in Tyrell's primal scent.

"Ahh, shiiit," were Tyrell's first words as he busted cum all over Kanika's lips and mouth. Her first reaction was to wipe it away and back off, but something took over and she licked him good. She was honored to have what was a part of him now be a part of her. Tyrell's eyes grew wide as she sucked her fingers, making sure not to miss one drop.

"You ain't never done no shit like that," he panted, his forehead covered with beads of sweat. "Where you learn that?"

Kanika felt embarrassed; she thought she was doing something good. "It was just how I was feeling, that's all. Did I do it wrong?"

Tyrell ran his hands through her hair and pulled her into his embrace. He smiled. "It was *too* damn good." He picked her up and took her to the king-size bed. "Now, let *me* show you how much I missed that ass," he said, lowering his body next to her. "Get on top."

Kanika mounted his face, covering his mouth with her pussy. Her hands gripped the cold iron bedposts as her pussy rode his mouth and tongue. He squeezed her ass, sticking a finger inside, making Kanika scream out in pleasure. Tyrell's mouth glistened with her juices as his tongue lapped her up. He flipped her over on her knees and expertly slipped his dick inside her wetness.

Holding on to her hips, he leaned over and played with her pussy.

"Fuck this pussy hard, harder," she begged as she pressed her face into the mattress and her ass higher into the air. She couldn't believe her own words, taking all of Tyrell's twelve inches. She shut her eyes tightly, hoping it wouldn't hurt.

Tyrell rammed into her harder, an inch or two still hanging out. He slapped her ass cheeks, making them vibrate like ripples in a stream.

"Damn this ass. Fat, nasty ass," Tyrell whispered, his thrusts deeper and harder. "You my bitch, right? Say that shit."

"I'm your bitch!" she said, and spread her legs more, giving Tyrell's fingers more play with her pussy. Her eyes rolled back into her head as he finger-fucked her at the same time.

"Awww. I'm gonna come; I'm coming!" Kanika moaned, as her knees began to shake, making her lose her balance. But that didn't stop Tyrell, who was still pumping his dick into her, both now flattened on their stomachs. Kanika's pussy erupted again in another surge of fluid. Tyrell timed his just right so they came together.

They both lay in the same position, not moving an inch, until they heard, "Room service?"

Tyrell sprinted out of the bed, butt naked, took care of the waiter, and came back with a tray of champagne and his face lit up with happiness. "We left the door open."

"I bet we gave him the best tips he ever got." Kanika laughed and locked herself in Tyrell's arms.

"I never want to lose you again. I want to take you home and marry you. Make you my lil wifey," he said, his gaze steady and sincere, like he was sucking her soul out.

She leaned her head against his chest and kissed the space between his bulging pecs. "I wanna be with you forever, too. I know Mommy would have wanted to see us get married."

"Fa' sho'," Tyrell said, kissing her forehead.

"How's the house? You didn't get rid of anything, did you?" Kanika asked. It pained her to ask about her home, a place she wasn't sure she'd see soon.

"Everything is fine and alive. That house don't need no more death." He pulled the tray toward them with the champagne, strawberries, and cheese platter. "Sometimes I look at myself and see death in my face. That shit scares me sometimes out of my sleep. I look old as shit and I'm only twenty-four."

"No, Tyrell," Kanika said, stroking his chin. She turned his face toward her. "You look good and healthy to me. All I see when I think of you are those big, brown eyes soaking me up. I see a man who wants to please everyone, and not just himself. I see my teacher, and my husband, when I look at you. There's nothin' that speaks of death to me."

Tyrell popped open the champagne and let its air out. "I wish I could see that in myself. But that's what I got my shorty for, right?" he said, putting a strawberry in his mouth as Kanika bit the other end of it.

Tyrell sucked on her fingers, taking two in his mouth at a time. "I could just put you on this tray right now," he said, controlling himself. "We gonna be making a lot of babies when we get married. I love you, boo."

"I love you, too." Kanika grasped his sturdy, tall body and hugged him as tight as she could. She kissed him as the tears slid down her cheeks to her lips. This was actually how she had imagined their reunion would be. It dawned on her just how much she really loved this man.

Then her cell phone went off. She darted around the room until she found it lying on the living-room floor in her bag. It was Saliq.

"Who that?" Tyrell said, pouring the Moët White Star into her glass.

"Nobody important," Kanika said, shutting it off. And she recognized that Saliq was not going to be that easy to get rid of.

On Friday morning they went horseback riding. Tyrell didn't know what he was doing, but Kanika showed him. She had taken lessons when she was younger. They rode their horses in a peaceful bliss. Before she left for her father's party, she and Tyrell had a candlelight dinner under the full Virginia moon and afterward made love. Kanika fucked Tyrell so hard that he would be asleep for the next several hours. After the party, she planned to come back and give him some more. She wanted to make sure he remembered who that dick belonged to and that he'd never forget it.

Twenty-one

Shon rented a mansion set on a plantation for his annual "homecoming" party, a bash for five hundred of his closest friends out on bail or good behavior, business associates, neighbors, and even several politicians. It reminded Kanika of Tony and Waleema's parties, where everyone came out to floss, to see and be seen. It reminded her of Tyrell and how good they'd look. The place was crawling with tall, monied, attractive men and the women who loved them.

Kanika was posted at the front of the large ballroom. Tiffany was there with Shanae, cutting her eyes at Kanika every chance she got. Kanika admitted that Tiffany looked nice, too, but she was squeezed into the purple Prada dress that Kanika had passed on.

Kanika was looking fierce, in her short red and gold shimmery D & G dress and Gucci heels. She glided through the crowd as her father introduced her to folks. "Nice to meet you," Kanika must have said a thousand times. "Thank you for coming." She noticed that there wasn't much she had to do but look fly and pretty. Something that came natural.

"Saliq is here," Shon said, slipping his arm around Kanika. She knew exactly why her father was stressing him and her. Shon thought if she got locked down by somebody, she would never leave Virginia. But Shon had no idea how determined Kanika was to get the hell outta there—eventually.

"Mr. Lieutenant," Shon said to Saliq, as he stood between the two. "Now you two can talk to each other and feel comfortable."

"We met at the club already, Daddy," Kanika said awkwardly.

Saliq brought his lips to her hand. "For a brief minute, but this is much better."

Kanika nodded, folding her arms behind her. She was so embarrassed for ignoring all his calls.

"I noticed you didn't call me back," Saliq said, blowing up her spot.

Her father just stood there, all up in their business. She wanted him to leave.

"I have to holla at you, Kanika," her father said.

She and her father moved a few feet away.

"If you need a nigga in your life, that is the one. You would never have to do anything but fuck him and stay looking good."

"So this is really about getting me and Saliq together?" she asked. "To hell with what I really want?"

"Don't look too deep into it. I wanted you to host

and, in the process, get to know all the big players out here. Especially if you plan to stay," he said, glowering at her.

"I don't have those kinds of plans. Please stop trying to run my fucking life. Damn!" Kanika said.

Shon hauled off and smacked the shit out of her in front of everyone. Kanika stared at him in shock. "Well, you may want to keep your options open, Ms. Thang." Shon put his cigar back in his mouth, puffed out a ring of smoke, and walked off.

No one said anything but continued carrying on with the party as if nothing had happened. She felt like a fool holding on to her face while everyone else smiled and danced around her. She was so angry she couldn't even move or cry.

Next thing she knew, Saliq was standing next to her. "Listen, let's go outside and get some fresh air," he said, protectively putting his arms around her. He snagged a glass of wine from the cocktail waitress and passed it to Kanika.

Kanika allowed Saliq to led her to the outdoor garden. She felt wobbly and disoriented.

"She'll learn to keep that stank attitude in New York next time," Tiffany said, with Shanae in tow, as they passed her.

"Whatever, bitch," Kanika said loud enough for Tiffany to hear her.

Kanika stood outside with Saliq, dumbfounded at how she had ended up in his arms anyway.

Saliq pulled her down onto a wooden bench. "You

know how your daddy gets sometimes. I mean, I'm sure he didn't mean it," Saliq said.

"This ain't the time to take up for him, Saliq. He's a true motherfucka."

Saliq ran his fingers across her collarbone. "You smell nice."

She knew he was trying to distract her. Kanika drank some more wine. Saliq's delicate touch was welcome. She closed her eyes. Right now, her head was spinning was so many thoughts, she needed comfort from anywhere.

"Too bad you got a man," he said.

She gripped her wineglass so hard she thought it would crack. She felt queasy.

"You wanna go somewhere?" she said, as she grabbed another glass of wine off another cocktail waitress's tray. Kanika wanted to get back at Tyrell and get away from everyone around her. Peaches, Tiffany, her father, even Tyrell all seemed to be fulfilling their own selfish desires. So why couldn't she? She was already feeling fucked up, and she thought, *Why not fuck shit up more?* Better to get the pain over with all at once. Maybe she'd get so lost in it, she wouldn't notice how much it hurt anymore.

Kanika and Saliq walked down a grassy hill to the lake below. Saliq laid his jacket down for Kanika to sit on as they looked at the silky black water.

"You cold?" Saliq asked, pulling her into him and brushing his nose behind her ears. She closed her eyes, imagining those lips were Tyrell's. But these were another man's, the second man she had ever gotten this close to. She wondered if he and Tyrell were the same in everything else.

Saliq's hands wandered over her breasts as he unbuttoned the top part of her dress. Kanika's first instinct was to stop him, but then Tyrell's sleeping face came before her.

She stuck her chest out and helped Saliq with the buttons. He sucked on her titties with his thick, juicy lips. His breath was hot and moist, turning her nipples hard like coins.

Saliq pushed his tongue between her lips. Kanika opened her mouth wide to welcome him. She heard him whispering something under his breath, but she couldn't understand. She felt a hardness pressing on her thigh. She reached down and felt the length of his dick, which was nowhere near the size of Tyrell's but still respectable.

Saliq scanned her naked breasts and traveled down to her thighs. He pulled her dress up.

"Oh!" Kanika gasped in the night. The night breeze made it feel ten degrees cooler, but the cool sensation and Saliq's hot tongue on her quivering pussy almost made her lose her mind. Both of her legs were cocked in the air as Saliq turned her pussy into dessert. Her face turned to the night sky above with the twinkling stars staring down at her with envy. A feeling of elevation came over her like the gentle waves hitting the rocks.

She urged him on with contorted facial expressions. The pink of his unusually long tongue drove her to another level of pleasure. His entire tongue covered her from her clit to her asshole.

"Oh God, Tyrell!" she said, her thighs shaking. She caught herself and gasped, but Saliq didn't seem to notice. He was too busy going to work on her.

When he was through, he planted gentle kisses on her pussy, leaving her in a state of bliss. He sat beside her and found her lips again.

"I was feeling you the first time I met you," he said, carefully pushing her bangs away from her face. "I don't care if you got a man; I want you all to myself."

"I'm not ready for all that yet," she said coldly, turning her back to him.

Saliq began nibbling on her neck. Suddenly a heavy weight sat in her stomach. She didn't know if it was the liquor or the beginning of a messy situation.

"Had fun?" Tyrell asked in the dark when Kanika walked in at 3:00 A.M. She was tipsy and tired. But a smile grew on her face when she saw the rose petals everywhere.

"Aww," she purred, sitting on his lap. "I love you." She began to kiss his neck, but he shoved her off.

"You smell like cologne," he said, turning on the lights in the hallway. "Get over here."

Kanika walked carefully to him near the bed. She was trying to be as sober as she could, but it wasn't working. She wrapped her arms around his waist, wanting him to look her in the eye. "I'm not drunk. I just had a sip of champagne and I was meeting a lot of people. Maybe that's why I smell like cologne."

He stiffened in her hold. He didn't even hold her back.

"Please, Tyrell," she said, looking up at the darkness of his eyes. "I need you to make love to me right now, baby. Right now." She rubbed his chest, pressing her body against his.

"If I ever catch a nigga with you—don't do it to me, Kanika," he said, slowly melting in her arms.

"Never, baby," she said, lying back on the bed. She took Tyrell's hands and moved them over her body, soothing the beast in Tyrell.

He helped her out of her dress. His love for Kanika was bigger than anything he had fantasized about. He felt drawn to her like a crackhead to his next hit. "I made a bath for you," he said.

"You getting in the tub with me," Kanika said, lowering her aching body into the bubbly, warm water.

"Not yet," Tyrell said, sitting on the edge of the tub. He wet a sponge and gently massaged the soap on her back into a lather.

"Mmmm," Kanika moaned as she rolled her neck around. Tyrell made her feel that whatever bad he did wasn't so bad after all. He loved only her, and it showed in his words and touch.

Tyrell continued to bathe her, then stopped to

massage her shoulders. He kissed her neck. Kanika stood up, and he lathered her ass, legs, and pussy.

"Looks like somebody needs a little trim," Tyrell said, taking out a razor from a pack on the sink.

Kanika laughed, a little embarrassed. "You wanna shave me?"

Tyrell sprayed some shaving lotion on her pussy and rubbed it in with some water around the hair.

Kanika spread her legs and he began to carefully shave her. She was nervous, but as she hiked one leg on the ledge of the tub she relaxed. Tyrell knew what he was doing. He shaved her skillfully and with the attention an artist gives to his masterpiece.

This was another form of trust and intimacy between them. Shit, she wouldn't let just anyone down there with a razor. And she had never experienced this before. They weren't in the heat of a steamy fuck session. Tyrell was showing her another form of his love and admiration. She was like his child, his angel, and his bitch all at the same time. She was his everything, and he was hers.

Twenty-two

Now that Shon was in New York, it was just Kanika, Peaches, and Tiffany at the house. It also had been three days since Tyrell left. Kanika felt like he took a part of her heart with him. He told her he'd send for her next time. But she didn't plan to wait on that. She was already making up her mind to do a pop-up visit on a moment's notice. She was his "main," his "wifey," his "number one," and where she came from that carried more weight than a five-carat diamond ring.

After a full day of classes, Kanika got a ride home with Shanae, who always made Kanika laugh for one reason or another.

"You know what, girl, I think we need to get something to eat, so I can get all in your business about Saliq," Shanae said as they walked to her car. "I saw the two of you in each other's face at the party."

"There ain't much to say. But I didn't eat any breakfast rushing out of the house to take this damn test. I bet I failed." Kanika inhaled deeply. Saliq was irrelevant at this point.

"I know I did fine. I studied for the last three weeks," Shanae boasted. "Oh, we should go to Burger Palace—"

As Shanae suggested some spots to eat, Kanika had an urge to call Tyrell. She needed some encouragement to get her worried mind off the test. She searched her bag for her cell and couldn't find it.

"What's wrong?" Shanae asked, as Kanika emptied her bag onto her lap.

"I can't find my fuckin' cell phone," she said, rubbing her temple. "Oh no, I think I musta forgot it at home. Damn!"

"So, if it's home, it's home. It's not like it's lost," Shanae said, trying to calm her down.

"Yes, but so is Tiffany. And I know she would try to pick it up if it rang to get all in my business." Kanika thought she was being foul talking about Tiffany to her friend, but she was so mad at herself, she didn't care. She made a silent request that Tyrell and Saliq had gotten short-term memory loss and forgetten her number.

"Let me get your ass home now." Shanae laughed. "Tiffany is my girl and all, but she got no shame in her game. When she wanna know something she's the Ghetto Columbo."

When Kanika walked into the house she heard a few female voices from the kitchen.

"Hello," Kanika said when she saw Tiffany and a skinny yellow-skinned woman with dark marks down her arms. Kanika had never seen this woman before, and she reminded her of the crackheads back home.

"Kanika, this is my mother, Gayle," Tiffany said, nodding to her mother and Kanika.

Gayle barely lifted her eyes to meet Kanika. It was like she was ashamed.

"Hello, Gayle," Kanika said, walking toward her. She held out her hand. Gayle smelled of old urine, and her jeans and T-shirt were oversize and dirty.

"Please, girl, it's not even that deep. My mama here for some money, now that Daddy is gone. He don't let her up in here because she be stealing," Tiffany said matter-of-factly.

Kanika dropped her bag to the ground and saw her cell phone sitting on the kitchen island seemingly untouched.

Gayle finally looked at Kanika. Her eyes clouded with hatred. "If it wasn't for your mother, I wouldn't be like this," she said between her teeth. "She destroyed any love he could've given me."

That was when Tiffany looked saddened.

"I'm sorry for what happened, but my mother was not responsible for your decisions," Kanika said, grabbing her cell phone. She checked for missed calls and voice mails, but she had none. That was out of the ordinary for her. Tiffany had definitely erased them, she thought.

Gayle glared at her. "Siddity bitch."

"Nice to meet you, too," Kanika said, clipping her cell phone to her jeans. She turned to Tiffany. "I'll talk to *you* later." Kanika gathered her things and walked up the steps as quietly as possible. Soon after, she heard the front door close.

When Tiffany reached Kanika's bedroom, she came in with one of her fake smiles. "How was school?"

"It was good. I'm just tired as hell," Kanika said.

"Tyrell called," Tiffany said in a teasing tone. "And Saliq."

The words hit Kanika on her back like stones. She spun around and marched toward Tiffany. "How the hell you know?"

"You were stupid enough to leave your cell," Tiffany said, blowing on her freshly painted red nails.

"You betta stay the fuck out of my business," Kanika said, her finger in Tiffany's face. "Don't play with me, Tiff."

"Oh, please, girl," Tiffany said, taking a few steps back. "What you all upset about? Is there a reason you should be upset?"

"What did Tyrell say?"

"He said he'll call you back. I called him Saliq by accident because they sound just alike."

Bitch! Bitch! Bitch! "You called him Saliq? That's

some foul ole shit, Tiffany. But exactly what I would expect a chick like you to do."

"Don't get mad at *me* if you ain't being honest with your man. And yes, I did tell him that Saliq was at the party, because he asked and I am not about to be lying to folks."

Kanika threw a look at Tiffany as if she wanted to pummel her face in. But then Kanika thought of Gayle. Tiffany was definitely going through her own shit, too.

"I'm going to bed." Kanika walked away leaving Tiffany still standing there.

Kanika went inside her bathroom, closed the door, and called Tyrell. She didn't know what his reaction was going to be, but it was up to her to make everything OK.

"Tyrell, it's me. You called?"

"Yeah, and some chick picked up the phone," he said in a cold voice that confirmed that he had spoken to Tiffany. "Talking about she thought I was some other nigga, Saliq. Who that?"

Kanika swallowed. "That's my father's partner. We may have talked once or twice." She was not the best liar.

"You fuckin'?" he asked.

"No, no, Tyrell, just listen. This is a friend of my father's, that's all."

She heard a sharp silence on the other end. But Tyrell wasn't one to get too riled up on the phone.

The next thing she knew he would be here with his Ruger and busting niggas down.

"Tyrell, Tiffany got some kind of beef with me. She'll say anything."

"But she was right, true?"

"Yeah, but I know how she is. Just trust me."

"I don't trust dem VA motherfuckas. And if he roll with your pops, that mean dat nigga gotta be thorough. Maybe he need to know you already taken."

"I told him, I did, and he respects that," Kanika said.

"'Cause whatever you kickin' to him, still got the nigga callin."

Kanika sat down in a wooden rocking chair by her bed as she kept the phone pressed to her ear. "Tyrell, I just want to come home. I just feel completely by myself. And I know you do, too" she said, envisioning Saliq's face in her pussy. A shiver shot down Kanika's spine.

There was a long silence on Tyrell's end and Kanika knew he was struggling not to lose it. Finally he said, "Regardless of what Tiffany said, if anyone ever tries to disrespect you in any way, you call me. Aight?"

"OK, but I'm good."

They hung up.

Tyrell had her back no matter what, she thought. And she had his. Not even suspicion implanted by another or stepping out on the side could get in the way. It was all for one, one for all. She wasn't going anywhere, and neither was he. It was like that loyalty her father was talking about a few months ago.

Twenty-three

Kanika slipped on some headphones to drown out all the noise coming from Tiffany's room next door. Peaches was asleep in the guest room downstairs. Kanika didn't know what was going on with her because lately that's all she did. She had been living with them for three weeks, with no plans to get a job or enroll in school. She was just Kanika's father's plaything, but with him being away now, Peaches acted like she had no motivation to do anything but eat, sleep, and shop.

She didn't have time to tell grown folks like Peaches how to live their life anymore. Thankfully, Kanika had other things to worry about. In a few days, she had a major math exam. She had done poorly on the first and wanted to make up for it with at least a B. It frustrated her to know that her favorite subject had turned into a major threat.

Kanika kicked the wall that separated hers from Tiffany's room. The music lowered a few decibels, and then it was turned off.

Ring. Ring.

"Girl, it's me. I know you studying and all, but me and Shanae is going to an all-girls spot tonight. You down?"

"I don't know. I got too much studying to do," Kanika said.

"You scared?" Tiffany laughed. "Didn't you grow up in a strip club?"

"Exactly. So that shit is not that exciting to me. So if you bitches can't think of anything else—" Kanika said, throwing it back at her.

"Hold on, I'ma come in there."

"Look, Tiffany—" Kanika said, trying to stop her. She wanted to squeeze in at least another half hour of studying. "I know you just want me to come so I can get all the liquor and pay for it, too. You like the juice, respect it."

Tiffany swung Kanika's door open. "Well, it do have its benefits. But why you got to get all deep about it?"

Kanika sighed and hung up the phone. She was thinking of Peaches. "It wouldn't be right to leave Peaches here by herself. Peaches!" Kanika called downstairs.

A few moments later, Peaches was at the door with a sour face.

Tiffany asked, "You wanna come with us to the strip club?"

"Nah," Peaches said, shaking her head. "Wake me up when you get back, Kanika. I want to talk to you."

"About what?"

Peaches shook her head and left.

"That bitch be moody," Tiffany ranted. "You know what, let me get my ass ready before you two bitches start fucking up my mood."

Kanika slammed her book shut.

Kanika, Tiffany, and Shanae arrived at Coco's around 2:00 A.M. Tiffany and Shanae knew the bouncer, the bartenders, and some of the men sitting around sipping beers. Kanika was used to her mama's spot, where everybody bowed to whoever were her special guests. Drinks, chips for tips, and even food were all on the house at the Kitty Lounge for any balla type who was worth his weight. Kanika frowned, looking around. She knew her mama would blow the lid off this place with her style.

There was a wraparound bar with dancers in all shapes and sizes dancing in the middle and young men giving them one-dollar tips. There was a small DJ booth in the corner that played the latest in booty-shaking songs from the South.

They stopped to talk to one guy in a jean suit with gold chains around his neck. He slipped something, which looked like money, into Tiffany's hand.

"What you wanna drink?" Tiffany asked, whipping out a stack of singles from her purse.

"Some Alizé with Henny," Kanika said, peering at the long legs of the women dancing nearby.

"Make that three!" Shanae said as Tiffany placed their orders.

As they waited for the drinks, Kanika made sure not to give any of the men eye contact. Hiding behind her big black shades, she managed to see the looks on some of their faces. Many seemed to be in a trance, eyes and faces lifted, with mouths slightly opened, petting and rubbing the asses and thighs of the dancers who came near them. Others seemed bored, depressed, as they focused more on their beers.

Shanae sipped her drink and waved a five-dollar bill at one of the girls. The girl smiled knowingly at Shanae and Tiffany like she knew what they wanted already. Kanika watched as the girl turned around, got down on her knees, and shook her rounded behind in Shanae's face. Tiffany's lips curled in a smirk as Shanae reached out and massaged the girl's ass with her superlong manicured nails. She squeezed the girl's flesh, which looked soft and supple, between her fingers. It looked like she was kneading dough, Kanika thought. Then Shanae slapped it once and slipped the money into the girl's purple G-string.

Kanika beckoned the same girl to her. She liked her more than the other girls for some reason. She was tall, slim, and looked friendly, with shiny shoulder-length black hair.

"Slap that ass!" Tiffany said to Kanika. "Yo, Diamond, show my sista a lil somethin'."

Diamond stood over Kanika dressed in a glitter-encrusted garter belt and did the Booty Clap. She popped her thick booty up and down, making the cheeks clap together. Kanika reached up and ran her hands across Diamond's silky skin. And with each touch Kanika felt herself get more engrossed in what she was doing. Tiffany and Shanae looked on through the smoky haze from a shared joint they were puffing on. Kanika slipped Diamond several dollars before she jiggled her way to the next tipper at the other end of the bar.

"You handled that chick pretty good, girl," Tiffany said, as she enticed another dancer with more money. "Wasn't your mama a stripper, too?"

Kanika cut her eyes at Tiffany. She sensed a thread of sarcasm in her voice. "Yes, and she *owned* her own club."

"But now I see where that freak side of you come from." Tiffany and Shanae laughed.

"Take notes, bitch," Kanika lashed back.

"Now you see how your mama got with a balla like Daddy back in dem days?" Tiffany said, turning her stool to face Kanika. "These chicks are straight gangsta when it come to getting with cats who got a long reach, and I ain't talkin' about the dick."

Kanika kept a stoic expression as she watched all the bodies around her bend and shake. All these cats in here had main girls or wives at home, thought

Kanika. It saddened her to know that her mother had done this. Kanika never really knew what drove her mother to dance. All she recollected was that her mama used to urge her to go to college. But then she remembered what had happened earlier in the summer when she sneaked her way into her mother's club and heard a dancer talking about her mother and another woman getting it on. Kanika could see here how a strip club could turn any woman out, and for the first time it occurred to her that maybe her mother was a straight-up bisexual.

"Girl, you OK?" Shanae said, stroking Kanika's back. "You look blue in the face."

"Maybe that drink is too strong. Let me help you wit' that," Tiffany said, sliding Kanika's half-finished drink over.

Kanika slid it back. "I am fine, y'all. I was just thinking about my mama and wondering if she liked dancing."

"She probably did," Tiffany said. "At a good club, you can make a thousand a week."

"Most of them be eating pussy, but they don't be gay," Shanae said, as they looked at two girls grinding their pussies together.

"All these chicks are bi," Tiffany said. "Just imagine being around naked women most of the day. All that ass and titties, bumping into each other, having to dance together, it's almost natural for that to happen."

What if I'm bisexual, too? Kanika thought. She actually enjoyed what she was seeing, but she couldn't see herself doing anything but tipping.

"You want some?" Tiffany asked, as she rolled another blunt with Shanae. Both of their eyes were nearly bloodshot with Alizé, Henny, and weed all in their systems.

"I'll pass," Kanika said, as she watched Tiffany sprinkle a white dust in the weed mixture.

"Daddy know you using that shit?" Kanika asked, surprised to see Tiffany handling coke.

"Look, this my lil shit I do on my downtime. I don't need nobody watching ova' my shoulder," Tiffany said, licking the edges of her blunt.

Kanika grew worried. "Tiffany, that's coke. Daddy would kill ya ass."

"Only if he finds out. You plan on telling him?"

Kanika waved away the smoke.

"My mama was a crackhead. I guess you think I'ma be one, too?" Tiffany smiled. "Girl, you got jokes fa' days!"

But Kanika wasn't joking. She knew that the apple didn't fall far from the street. And it would only take a little less weed for Tiffany to start snorting straight coke.

After Tiffany and Shanae shared the joint and another round of drinks, everyone was ready to leave. But Tiffany and Shanae were in no condition.

"Where Dexter at? Didn't he drive tonight?" Shanae slurred.

"Who Dexter?" Kanika asked, knowing she was the only one in her right mind at this point.

Tiffany only grunted as she puffed away on a new joint, and slipped a one-dollar bill in a woman's bra.

"I can drive your car," Kanika said to Tiffany, holding her hand out for the keys.

"You can drive alone. Because we gonna get a ride with Dexter," Shanae said.

"Why?"

Tiffany finally managed to put a sentence together. "We usually have our own little after party at the house whenever Daddy be gone."

Kanika grabbed the car keys from Tiffany's hand. "I'll see y'all at the house." On her way out, Kanika looked back. She saw Tiffany slide off the bar stool and carefully walk through the crowd to Dexter, who was talking to several women. Kanika knew it was him by how Tiffany had her hands all over him. He was the same guy who had slipped her the money.

Kanika reached home before everyone else. She had it in her to call Tyrell. But the alcohol had made her drowsy, too. She got into bed with just a T-shirt and her panties and turned on the fan full blast. That talk with Peaches would have to wait until the morning, she thought. In minutes, she was sound asleep.

Two hours later, Kanika woke up with a dry, parched throat. She walked downstairs to the kitchen and fixed herself a glass of apple juice. When she flipped the lights on, she saw panties, boxers, jeans, and bras lying around the floor, with pieces scattered on the steps.

It looked like someone had emptied their dresser drawer on the ground. There were specks of white dust and weed on the glass coffee table, too. Kanika walked slowly back up the steps and stopped at Peaches' room. She was snoring. Kanika went up another flight and heard several moans coming from Tiffany's room. She tiptoed to her door and through the slit saw three naked chocolate bodies packed on top of one another like a sandwich. Kanika's mouth opened slightly as her eyes widened. Tiffany and Shanae were humping each other, and Dexter was on top with his dick in Shanae's ass. Kanika gingerly sipped her juice as she watched the live freak show. It reminded her of the few times she caught her mother and Tony getting their freak on. She wasn't about to interrupt anyone's groove, because from the looks of it no children were involved.

There was only a small amount of light in the room supplied by a lamp on Tiffany's desk. But Kanika could see and smell everything. They changed positions, and Tiffany and Shanae slid down and sucked on Dexter's dick, taking turns. Dexter's moans filled Kanika's ears as he held Tiffany's and Shanae's faces between his legs. Kanika got a real good look at Dexter. He was a finely sculpted specimen, not necessarily the most handsome but definitely in shape, with large hands that scooped Shanae and Tiffany up like babies. Kanika caught

Dexter's eye, and she didn't blink. Neither did he. She thought he was daring her to join them or teasing her, as she swore she saw a smirk. He lay on his back and motioned for Tiffany to sit on top of his dick while Shanae sat on his face. That was when Kanika walked back to her room, where their moans kept her up until it was over thirty minutes later.

She heard Dexter leaving with Shanae soon after. As Kanika spied from the top of the stairs, he slipped Tiffany a small plastic bag of tiny white rocks. She had her own secret world, and Kanika wanted nothing to do with it.

Twenty-four

Two days later, Kanika finally caught up with Peaches. When Kanika walked in from school she cornered her in the living room.

"I know you been wanting to talk, but you know I've been busy," Kanika said, sitting on the white leather couch. Peaches was laid out on the L-shaped sofa watching a talk show.

Peaches turned the TV off. "I don't know how to say this."

"Is it about my daddy?" Kanika said, glancing at Peaches, who was looking nervous.

"It is. I just didn't think it would go this far."

Kanika walked over to Peaches and sat beside her. She put her hand on her shoulder. "Girl, if you want me to tell him that this ain't for you I will. I'm glad you are coming to your senses. You can do a lot better than my father."

Peaches kept her eyes down. "I'm having his baby."

Kanika snatched her hand away and stared at Peaches in disbelief. She felt like she was suffocating.

Peaches had a sick, sarcastic smile on her face. "At least it ain't Tyrell's."

Kanika laughed. "Excuse me? I must be hearing things."

"I had sex with Tyrell, Kanika; you might as well know. But it wasn't his fault."

Kanika's mouth stayed open long enough for her tongue to dry. She felt like she had been punched in the chest. She couldn't breathe.

"Kanika?" Peaches asked, looking alarmed.

All Kanika saw was that sick pitiful smile again. She knew Peaches had finally gone crazy. "You are that obsessed with me that you fucked my father and now my man? What are you trying to do, destroy my fucking life?" Kanika was so enraged that her eyes began to burn from keeping them open for so long without blinking.

Unmoved, Peaches said plainly, "You got everything."

Kanika balled up her fists and wanted to pound Peaches to a bloody mound. But she thought of her mother. And Waleema would get the facts first. "What the fuck happened between you two?"

"I thought he would have told you by now," Peaches said, shaking her head. "Niggas ain't shit."

Kanika went to her bedside table, opened the drawer, took out her loaded .45 Tyrell gave her, turned around, and pointed it at Peaches' head. "Bitch, you better fucking speak up, or I will cap you in your ass, I don't care if you pregnant or not," she said, her hands feeling sweaty. She felt crazy enough that she would actually shoot somebody, herself or Peaches.

"Kanika, please," Peaches said, looking terrified. "I did it because, I don't know, I thought he was gonna be fucking anyway, but probably some bitch you hated; at least you know who he was with—"

Kanika felt rage burning her from the inside out. It took all she had not to blow a hole in Peaches' head. Instead she said, "You always hated me, Peaches, behind that fake-ass smile. Now you pregnant by my daddy," Kanika continued in a low, disturbing voice. "This is my family you messing with. I would kill you, but you ain't even worth it."

"Kanika, I need your help. I can't have this baby alone." Peaches cried harder.

"You must be out of your fuckin' mind. Pack your shit and get out," she said, waving her gun. "I want you out before the sunset."

About ten minutes before the day blended into night, Peaches was gone.

Kanika called Tyrell as soon as the door shut behind Peaches. She was going to come from the left at him. He wouldn't have any idea that she was about to reveal what she had learned. She knew niggas would eventually dig their own graves.

"Peaches is pregnant," she said calmly as soon as he picked up.

She could hear him holding his breath. "What?" Tyrell choked out. "Did she say whose it is?"

"My daddy's, that's whose. He's been fucking her since she got here," Kanika said, studying her nails.

Tyrell let out a heavy sigh of relief. "Good."

"What you mean, good, nigga? That's my damn father," Kanika said.

"I mean good that it's not more serious."

"I'm close to catching a murder charge, for real."

"Peaches definitely trying to get over. She always the one scheming on a nigga."

"And how would you know?" Kanika said, dead serious.

"What you mean?" Tyrell asked, getting jittery again.

"Peaches told me everything, Tyrell," Kanika said, her voice devoid of any emotion. It was like she was reading from a script. Kanika heard Tyrell breathing heavily.

"Aight, aight," he said, his voice shaky. "But let me tell you, I swear none of this was planned. She called me up. She told me you wanted her to make sure I was eating right."

"Oh really?" Kanika said, rage starting to build in her voice.

"Just listen," Tyrell said; his voice begged to be heard. "I went by because she said her mom had fixed some grub. But, her moms wasn't there. Then she started popping some shit about how you meeting mad people, partying; she made a nigga feel like you was out there, about to start a new life without me—at least for a moment."

"Oh, so you fucked her because of me?"

"No, she seduced a brother. She musta put some shit in my food. She grabbed my hand. Put it on her ass, and all that. Yo—" Tyrell broke down. "I'm sorry. I swear it didn't hit me till it was over. It was exactly three minutes. We used protection. Please believe it."

"Did you ever plan to tell me?"

He didn't answer at first. He finally said, "At some point. I was just hoping by then you would love me a little more."

Kanika closed her eyes. "Tyrell, I did love you. I couldn't have loved you any more. You were my everything."

Tyrell knew he was losing her and began to panic. "I'm so sorry. I feel like a fool to keep saying it. But everything just kind of happened. I was hurt, confused, weak. I hate that ho!" he said.

Kanika didn't say anything.

"I'll do what I have to, baby. Anything. Just tell me what to do," he pleaded. "But don't say good-bye."

Kanika wanted to be held tight by Tyrell, even if what he was saying was a lie. She needed him like she needed air. But if she stayed it would be her heart, her very spirit that would die. She believed that Tyrell loved her, but she needed him to love himself, too, if they were going to be together.

"Good-bye, Tyrell," she said and hung up the phone just as he screamed her name.

Twenty-five

A week passed. The word was that Peaches hadn't returned to New York City but was in Virginia chillin' with family. Kanika felt haunted but at least she wasn't in New York City, near Tyrell. When she told Tiffany about Peaches' pregnancy, Tiffany had just shrugged it off. It was almost as if Tiffany were a shell, with no true feelings, and it hurt Kanika that she had no one in the house to confide in. On top of that frustration, she had been getting Cs on most of her papers and her grades were slipping. Tyrell called her at least ten times a day. Saliq become her perfect distraction, taking her out, making her feel special, like the princess she always had been. And whatever else happened—happened.

On Thursday evening, Saliq took Kanika out to the movies. She had failed her big economics exam a few days ago. With being away from home and the drama with Peaches and her daddy, it was hard to focus lately.

"I got somethin' to wet your tongue," Saliq leaned over and said in her ear as they watched the movie previews.

"Like what?" Kanika asked.

He pulled out a brown paper bag from his jacket.

"A little Alizé," he said, holding a small bottle. He pulled out two plastic martini cups from another bag. "Everything I do, I do it in style."

Kanika held the bottle and read the label. It was a handy little bottle of Gold Passion, one of her mother's favorites. Saliq poured the yellow drink into their respective cups as a few couples seated around them stole glances.

"This is nice and cold," Kanika said, licking her lips. "Where'd you get this?"

"I got my way of doing things," he said, holding up the cup like he was giving a toast. "Besides, I wanted to make this evening special. Drink a little Alizé, watch a little movie, eat good later. If we was at my place I'd hook it up with some Henny and Hypnotiq."

"This is definitely unique," Kanika said, holding her cup. They both turned their attention to the darkening screen as their movie began to run.

About fifteen minutes into the flick, Kanika felt Saliq's hands moving up her Moschino jeans to the warm spot between her thighs. She didn't move and parted her legs slightly. There was a pulsating feel down there that had to do with getting none for weeks. With Tyrell, she was used to some action at least once a day. Saliq left his hand on the inside of her thigh as if he was teasing her with the possibility of more.

"You like the movie?" he asked, putting his arm across her shoulders.

"It's a little confusing, but Denzel is always good." As Saliq massaged her shoulder she began to feel like tonight was going to be a long, interesting evening. His hand was powerful, and he reached deep into her skin like he wanted to climb inside her. She did like him but hoped she would be able to keep things from going too far. By midway through the movie, Saliq was already sniffing around her neck and ears.

After the movie, they went for drinks at an upscale bar in Virginia Beach called Perks. The hostess sat them down at one of the best tables, tucked away in the corner with a view of the sunset over the water. Saliq ordered them a platter of baked clams, champagne, and crispy prawns. There wasn't anything Kanika needed that Saliq hadn't already provided, just like Tyrell.

"How you like your baked clams?" He engulfed the succulent meat from the shell in his mouth.

"Baked clams are my favorite," Kanika said, picking at hers with a fork. "I just don't know how to eat them, I guess."

"You supposed to suck on it. Put your mouth all around it," he said, demonstrating with another clam.

Kanika watched him suck out the meat again and was mesmerized by the movement of his mouth. His lips were evenly brown and thick. She tried it. "Mmmm, this is good," she said, her mouth full.

"It is," he said, laughing. "But I love the part where I suck the meat out of the shell."

Kanika smiled shyly at his sexual hint. She didn't mind his boldness and liked the feeling of being desired sexually. And Saliq was as fine as they came.

"So, you really wearing the hell outta them jeans," he said. "You look bad."

Kanika giggled as she reached for her third glass of Moët. "Thank my mama; don't thank me," she said, nodding her head to the side. She had planned to wear a fitted dress she had been saving for when Tyrell came into town, but it was already October and the nights were getting too cool.

Saliq poured himself another glass of Moët and refilled her glass with a little more. Already Kanika was feeling light and tipsy. The champagne tasted cold, crisp, and sweet with the few drops of Grand Marnier he dropped in from his flask.

Kanika got home at four in the morning.

"I hope you had a good time tonight. I know I did," Saliq said, his lips forming a sumptuous smile, at her door. He encircled Kanika's waist with one arm.

"I did, too," she said, smiling.

He kissed her. In one quick moment, their tongues danced in and out of each other's mouths. Kanika dropped her arms down and let Saliq make love to her mouth.

He placed his index finger on her lips. "Let me be that man in your life." His hands slid down to her behind. "I got some bigger and better things planned for you. You just ride with me on this one," he said, bending down to kiss her lips again.

Kanika closed her eyes and kissed him back. There was something about Saliq that made her body ache to be touched.

"I don't know about riding with you. The way my mom went down is not how I want to live my life. Though it's in *me,* I don't want to be in *it,*" she told him.

"Hold up; where all that coming from? You ain't judging a nigga, are you?" He grimaced.

"No, no, it's not that," Kanika said, taking his hand and sitting on the swinging bench. "It's just I'm scared still because of what happened to my family. I'm sure my daddy told you."

"Yeah, he did. And I was really feeling that because my pops went down, too, but he doing life, so he might as well be dead. That is why I gotta redeem his name. Never thought of backing down."

Kanika wanted to explain her fears, but she swallowed her words. "I guess I just miss home," she said, standing up.

"Well, sounds like you thinking about all the wrong things. If a nigga said he got you, he got you. No need to keep guessing," he said. "Fuck that nigga you used to be with. I'm here with you, where he should be."

Kanika thought about how Tyrell had said the same things before and now they were broken up.

That night she dreamed of Tyrell. Every part of her wanted him back. She needed to hear his voice. He was still calling her like twelve times today. His messages were filled with so much sadness, she just wanted to call him up and forgive him. She wanted to put this all behind her. *Why, Tyrell?* A little piece of the love she had for him died when he told her about Peaches. But she was still in love, still caught up. She'd die for him, and she knew, in a heartbeat, he'd die for her.

But she could never trust him again, and that destroyed her very being.

Twenty-six

The next day Kanika slept in and woke up to the sound of the doorbell ringing. It was Saliq.

He had a set of Louis Vuitton duffel bags. One packed, one empty. He handed her the empty one. "Fill this motherfucka up. We going on a little getaway."

In a few hours, Kanika was standing outside on the balcony of their penthouse suite at the Marriott in Virginia Beach. Saliq was sprawled out on a lounge chair staring up at the sky. Kanika saw this time away as a way to get some questions answered, despite Saliq's own motives.

He moved up behind her, and nestled his face in her neck. "Mmm, you smell so good," he said, then moved to nibble on her lobe.

"Can I ask you something?" she said, looking at the sunset.

"Anything," he murmured.

"What is my daddy really doing in New York?"

Slowly, he led her inside the room and closed the blinds. Kanika was nervous as hell. But it was cool.

"Why you ask?" he said, sitting on the couch.

"Just curious." She stepped between his legs and traced his goatee with her long nails. She slid her fingers over his thick, delicious lips. She felt him become hard and rise against her leg.

"He supposed to be looking into something. He heard some street rumor about who killed your moms," he said, rubbing her thighs.

"Really?" Her heart hurt, she wanted Tyrell to be holding her, touching her. But she didn't want to get all emotional right now. She needed information. "Is that all?"

"Your daddy know who killed your mama," he said and planted a big kiss on her lips. "But whoever did, ain't gonna get their hands on you—ever."

Saliq unbuttoned her fitted, pink blouse and unfastened her bra. She prayed that he didn't feel how hard her heart was pounding, as he licked her nipples. But slowly, she did relax and blocked out what she was feeling. Saliq handled her gently and suckled on her nipples until her pussy overflowed. He slid down the round, pushed her shorts to one side and licked her pussy with the eagerness of a kitten. Kanika bent her legs back to her shoulder and began to cry silently. They made love all weekend. The pleasure took over every ounce of pain, confusion, and doubt she had.

Twenty-seven

"Coming from somewhere?" Kanika's father asked as he stood at the doorway of her bedroom. She had just gotten back home from being with Saliq. Kanika didn't even hear him knock. She covered her breasts, not sure why, which were only covered by the thin fabric of her wife beater. She thought her father should have knocked. As a grown woman, she had a right to her privacy, and her fully developed body wasn't something she could easily downplay.

"Daddy, you could have knocked before you just busted in," Kanika said, grabbing her robe. She wanted to talk to him, but she could tell this was not the time.

"You built just like your mama. I already done seen what ya got. No need to hide from your ole pops," he slurred in his liquored breath. She thought he must have been drinking on his own for a while.

He walked toward her. "Damn, you been eatin' grits all ya life?" He laughed.

Kanika felt naked, though by this time she was fully covered. Her father's reaction to her body made her feel dirty and violated. He had this look in his eyes that made her stand several feet away from him.

"Can you please leave?" she asked, her hand over her chest.

"Your mama used to bring home thousands a night with a body like that," he said, taking a swig from his pewter flask. "Damn, I miss her. Having you around is like being with her again."

By this time, her father's eyes were a yellowish-red, soaking up every inch of her. "Too bad for Tyrell. I know he misses you."

"I ain't Mommy, for your information. I'm my own woman," Kanika said. "And how the hell you know about me and Tyrell?"

"And I know about you and Saliq." He snickered. "Just like your mama," he said, wiping his mouth. "That bitch lost her faith in me. She didn't think I had what it took to take care of her. Look at me now," he said, doing a drunken dance.

"Yeah, Mommy sure missed out," Kanika said, rolling her eyes at him. "You need to stay out my business with Tyrell."

Before she could roll her eyes back down, a hard hand landed on the right side of her face. "Kanika, as big as you are, I'll beat you like you stole some-thing," he said, shaking his hand off from the impact. "Ya hear me? I'll be all up in your business till I die."

"You got Peaches pregnant," Kanika said, holding her burning cheek. "How could you?" The thought to strike back like her mom would do occurred to her. But she was more afraid of her father than she had ever been of any other man. It didn't sadden her that she got hit; what saddened her was that she felt she deserved it.

Her father erupted in laughter. "That is one crazy ho. Let's just say I fixed that lil problem."

"What you do?" Kanika was afraid to ask.

"She ain't pregnant no more; that's all you need to know."

Kanika didn't need to know any more. He had either given Peaches the money to abort or beaten the baby out of her. Strangely enough, Kanika felt relieved.

"So anyway, like I was saying," her father commenced, as he sat down on the bed. "Where you coming from? You was with Saliq?"

Her hand was still on her stinging, swollen face. "I packed up some bags of old summer clothes. That's all."

"Good, because I don't want you leaving this house without letting me know," he said, sticking his flask in his back pocket.

Twenty-eight

Tyrell lay in the hotel bed as he thought about Kanika with another man. Her father had told him to come down in hopes of patching things up with Kanika. He didn't really trust her father, but he was desperate. His blood boiled just thinking of her with another man. To him, Kanika was the only innocence he knew. She represented everything that was pure and good to him. She was the only thing that made him want to change his life. He knew some cat was hollering. She basically told him months ago, but he never thought it would end like this. Her telling him about another man made him feel at fault because he was supposed to be her protector. He thought she wouldn't have had to go to another man for attention if he was the man he promised her he could be.

Whatever the case, he believed that Kanika belonged to him even though she broke up with him. He hadn't exactly been a saint, but his heart lay with her only. If he ever lost Kanika, he thought, it would be like losing himself or his future. He never quite understood the power she had over him or the love he had for her until she was gone. The way he felt for her shook him because it meant he was giving up his power, his control. He'd done everything right up until this point to ensure a happy future for both of them except one thing. The one thing that made him wake up from his sleep in a cold sweat, not able to move. That thing could tear Kanika away from him for good. And he planned to take it to his grave—if he could.

"Yeah?" Tyrell said, as he picked up an unidentified call on his cell. Kanika was supposed to be calling him after she was through with Saliq.

"This is Kanika's father. Kanika said she'd meet you at the house. But you gotta get down here now."

Tyrell rubbed his growing goatee. Her father's tone reeked of self-importance. "Can I talk to her?" Tyrell asked. Something seemed out. But, whatever, he thought.

"No, nigga. She's here. You either come or forget it," Shon said. Tyrell walked over to the minibar and poured himself some Hennessy.

Kanika's father said in a sarcastic manner, "Plus, I have a few important things to say to each you. *Man-to-man*. I'm at 145 Jamestown Road, right outside Hampton."

Tyrell swallowed his drink in one straight shot. "I'll be there in about an hour," he said, and hung up.

He threw on his jeans, a light gray sweater, and stuck his Ruger with a twenty-one-shot clip in his waist belt. He thought about leaving it, but he traveled with it all the time. It would like leaving home without his wallet.

As Tyrell drove down the Virginia highway, his street instinct told him to stay on-point. He had heard about her father since he was a kid on the come-up. Shon had the game for almost twelve years in Virginia. And Tyrell did have respect for him but was aware that he was shady. He wasn't about to sleep on him. But if it meant risking all that just to have a talk with Kanika, so be it, he thought.

"Is Mr. Jones here?" Tyrell said to a young woman who answered the door.

"Oh, you Tyrell?" she said, popping her gum hard. "You cute."

"Can I come in?" he asked, entering. "You Tiffany?"

"Yeah," she said, grabbing his hand. "Mmm, you are chocolaty and fine. If you were a cookie, I'd dip you in some milk, and swallow you whole." Tiffany smiled, flirtatiously batting her eyelashes at him.

"Aight." Tyrell smiled uncomfortably at Tiffany's overt friendliness. She had one of his arms locked into hers, her ample breasts exposed in a tight orange midriff top that showed her flabby belly. "Is Kanika around?" He slowly slipped his arm out of her grip.

She grabbed it again, squeezing his muscles. "She

is out with this dude. You may know him. But my daddy's expecting you," she said, walking him to the kitchen.

"Nah, thanks," Tyrell said, holding his head down. He smelled Kanika and was happy just to be this close. Everything looked like it was made out of porcelain, he thought. Pure, white leather furniture and cream colored walls. From a dark oil painting of Kanika's father that sat above the steps to the L-shaped white Italian sofa set, the house looked like it was fit for a king.

Tyrell stood at the kitchen doorway counting the minutes to when he'd hear from Kanika. He didn't care who she was with, because he knew where her heart belonged. He made sure there was at least three feet between him and Tiffany, but she kept inching closer. "So you think your pops ready to talk now?" He wanted to do what he had to do to get to Kanika.

"*I* am," she said, gliding over to him, face-to-face. Tiffany reached up and rubbed Tyrell's broad shoulders. "What you see in Kanika? She ain't that angel you think she is."

"Get off me, yo," he said, looking dead into Tiffany's face. He shrugged her arms off him, but Tiffany slipped her hands down to his belt buckle.

"I can tell you holding a big ole dick in dem jeans. Let me take a look," Tiffany said, licking her lips. She tugged on his belt buckle and got on her knees.

"Yo, fall back," Tyrell said, pushing her hands off him. "You supposed to be Kanika's sister?"

With a smirk plastered across her heavily painted purple lips, she turned around, pulled down her shorts, and leaned over the kitchen table. "Come on, just stick that big dick in my ass. I bet Kanika don't let you do that." Her hands spread her brown ass cheeks apart, teasing Tyrell to give it a try.

Tyrell thought about kicking Tiffany right in her ass for playing his woman. But he couldn't be bothered. Tiffany was someone who was trying to prove something, and he wasn't about to get caught out there.

"Fuck your tar black ass!" he heard Tiffany shout behind him as he left the kitchen.

Tyrell wanted to get as far away from the kitchen as possible. All he needed was Shon to accuse him of seducing Tiffany. He sat down on one of the leather couches in the living room. He bowed his head in a quiet prayer. He didn't know what he was saying, but he asked for guidance and protection.

"Tyrell," a booming voice said from above. Tyrell looked up and saw Kanika's father walking ever so slowly down the steps. He had a cigar dangling from his lips.

Tyrell stood up and waited till Shon approached him. "Hello, Mr. Jones."

"Yeah, yeah. No need to be all businesslike. Just be yourself, man," Shon said, blowing small circles of smoke as he sat down across from him.

"Well, I like to consider myself businesslike most of the time," Tyrell said, sitting down. "My business is my life."

"That is the truth," Shon said, taking a big drag from his cigar. "You know, my baby girl is real messed up over this."

"I told Kanika, I would do anything to take it back." Tyrell looked around the room to make sure they were alone. He saw the barrel of a 9 mm peeking from the inside of Kanika's father's jacket. "I'm sorry."

"Hey, man, you wanna drink? That's so rude of me," Shon said with a wicked smile. "Tiffany!"

Tyrell huffed, "No, thanks, Mr. Jones." He didn't want to see Tiffany again. But he felt like he had no choice. Shon had an idea how he wanted this meeting to go, so Tyrell would let him run the show.

"Fix us some drinks. A little Henny and Coke. Make mine with no ice," he ordered Tiffany, who rolled her eyes at Tyrell repeatedly, then disappeared into the kitchen. Tyrell thought how he didn't want to drink anything Tiffany made for him even if his life depended on it.

"Mr. Jones, I had said I wanted to talk about Kanika. I wanna take her back to New York and marry her." You said you may be able to talk to her for me."

"Oh, shit, this drink got too much fucking soda. Make me another one," Shon said to Tiffany, who, after handing Tyrell his drink, sauntered back into the kitchen.

Tyrell just set his drink on the glass coffee table.

"You were saying?" Shon said with a mocking grin.

Tyrell looked at him and wondered whether he was taking him serious or not. *Is he even listening?* Tyrell thought.

"I said I wanna marry Kanika," he said.

Tiffany gave her father the drink. He sipped it a few times before answering Tyrell, asking, "You sure you finish sowing your wild oats?"

Tyrell laughed nervously. "I love her to death. All I wanna do is make her happy."

Tiffany vanished up the steps, sensing what was about to go down.

"You were just being a man, Tyrell, I know. Things happen." Shon opened his black leather blazer. "You see this," he said, referring to the 9 mm. This is what makes me a man. And if anyone ever crossed me or my family—well, you know."

Tyrell glanced at the gun and then Shon. He didn't know what his point was, but it made him insanely uncomfortable. He discreetly moved his own hand across his waist to feel his piece. He pleaded in his head with God to let him not use it, even if he had to.

Tyrell good-humoredly held his hands up. "Mr. Jones. I don't want no problems. I thought it would just be a good idea to come to you like a man."

Shon rose from his seat and belted out a fake laugh. "I know more about your black ass than you know," he sneered. He pulled a long drag from his cigar.

Tyrell bit down on his lip. The room was air-conditioned, but he felt like it was one hundred degrees. "Like what?" he asked, somewhat pissed at her father's attitude.

"You killed my baby girl's mother. The woman I used to love. You ripped Kanika's world apart because your ass don't know how to order a hit," Shon said, strolling toward Tyrell. "That bitch Sharnell is one of my connects' sister. Remember her?"

Tyrell wanted to stand, but his legs were frozen. His head felt like it was stuck in the mouth of a wrench. The words were stuck in his throat. He wanted to deny it. This was all a setup, he realized.

"Well?" Shon asked, now standing over Tyrell.

Tyrell leaped off the couch and faced Kanika's father toe-to-toe. "I clipped them niggas who did that. *They* fucked up."

"Come on." Shon laughed. "You killed Waleema, man. Even if you didn't pull the trigger. That some shit you can't keep to ya self. Your secret is safe, if you never contact Kanika again."

Tyrell looked at Shon smiling and puffing away at his cigar. It looked like he was taking more pleasure in confronting Tyrell rather than trying to find out what really happened. But Tyrell knew there was no explanation he could give anyone about his mistake, especially Kanika. The thought of her knowing sent a sudden panic through him.

"I gotta go," he said, sweeping past Shon. But when he got to the door, Shon had a gun to his neck.

"Listen, nigga. Turn around and sit your ass back down. You wanted to talk man-to-man. Now handle yours," he said, shoving Tyrell back to the couch with the barrel of his gun.

Tyrell used one of his wrestling moves from high school to get Shon in a headlock. He threw him on the couch, pulled out his .45, and pressed it to his skull.

They both had their guns drawn at each other. Tyrell held the gun steady at point-blank range.

"So now you gonna kill Kanika's daddy," Shon said, unmoved by Tyrell's tactic. He waved his gun in Tyrell's face. "Go ahead, shoot me."

Tyrell's wet palms shook, making the gun feel slippery in his grasp. "Kanika ain't never gonna know. I never meant it. It was just supposed to be for Tony. Mad niggas was getting clipped because of him. Some dudes came out from St. Louis, did the job, but Waleema was with him. She got caught in the middle. I was nowhere around." The sweat trickled down the sides of Tyrell's shaved head; his eyes burned as he fought back tears.

Shon cocked his heat. "There's no way you leaving here with your life, Tyrell, let alone Kanika."

Twenty-nine

On the other side of town, Kanika was at Saliq's apartment.

She rehearsed in her head what she wanted to say. She needed a clean break. She really liked Saliq, but she wasn't ready for anyone new. She'd rather be alone and do her own thing. Get herself together. Be her own woman without a man calling the shots. She couldn't risk getting hurt again.

"You know how long I been trying to reach you?" Saliq said as soon as he opened his door. "Where you been?"

Kanika walked by him slowly despite his already-charged attitude, "I was thinking. I had to take some time for myself, after our weekend." The smell of weed permeated the air and made her feel nauseous. "We need to talk *now*."

"Mmmm," Saliq said, walking up to her and

fiddling with the strap of her green tank top. "How about we talk after I hit that?"

"Come on, Saliq," Kanika said, knocking his hand off her shoulder. "I'm serious."

"So am I." He slapped her backside. "Let me hit that real quick. I couldn't stop thinking about you since our weekend."

Kanika immediately regretted the weekend. She had a good time, but felt she was leading him on.

"How a man supposed to act with you looking all good, smelling good?" he said, pulling her arm in the direction of his bedroom. Then his cell phone went off.

Kanika breathed a deep sigh of relief.

After fifteen minutes, Saliq was still on his cell going back and forth with one of his partners. Kanika began to get impatient, because she wanted to get this done. She wanted to be free.

"Saliq?" she said, tapping her watch. "I gotta go and we need to talk."

Saliq hurriedly ended his call. "Listen, I want you to move in with me," he said, caressing her face.

Kanika thought he was delusional.

"Saliq!" she said. "I am not your woman. I'm not ready for anything serious."

"Well, can we talk about that later?" He circled his hands around her tiny waist, sliding them down to her fat behind.

She wiggled out of his embrace. "Saliq, I need you to listen to me."

Saliq lifted her up and laid her across his bed. She didn't want to go there with him, but she felt guilty. She had caused this. All of this could have been avoided if she had been honest from the start. She couldn't replace Tyrell with Saliq. But she opened her legs, and let Saliq search her with his hands and mouth. He ate her out like he wanted to know all her secrets, then he fucked her like she stole his money.

"Slow down, Saliq," Kanika said, gasping for air.

"Get your legs up higher," he ordered, as he banged into her. He nearly buried her in the mattress.

"Ohhh, Saliq! Oh God," she said, her insides waiting to explode for the first time since Tyrell. The sex was better than it had been the first time. He seemed to be fucking her with anger, and she'd rather he got it out that way than any other way.

He stuck his tongue in her ear, biting the edges. "You want that nigga Tyrell, don't you?" he asked, while he fucked her.

She looked up at him, her arms around his shoulders, in a sexual haze. "I do, I do . . ."

Saliq threw her legs over his shoulder, painfully contorting her body like pretzel. "Well, you might as well get used to this. Because your daddy got that nigga. Soon to be dead, nigga—" he panted.

Kanika stared up at him in shock. "What?" she said, but he just smiled and continued to pound inside her. Kanika tried to push Saliq off her, but he was solid as a rock. Panic threatened to overtake her.

Tyrell in Shon's hands meant somebody was gonna die!

"Get off me!" she said, biting the hell out of Saliq's neck.

He shot up, grabbing his bloody neck. "Bitch, you crazy?"

Kanika scrambled out of bed, and grabbed her clothes. She needed to get the hell up out of there and get back to the house. She quickly slipped into her clothes while Saliq continued to rant and rave. She charged to the door.

"You ain't going nowhere, bitch!" Saliq said, picking up her petite body and throwing it against the bed. "I ain't come yet."

Kanika flew at him, nearly scratching his eyes out. He punched her in the jaw, splitting her bottom lip.

They both wrestled with each other, until Saliq pinned her down.

"I knew you was gonna come up here all Ms. High-and-Mighty telling me you don't want me! I was waiting for you to mention that nigga!" he shouted, spit flying out of his mouth. He punched her again and Kanika lay there, stunned, while blood oozed from her lip.

Saliq, still naked, got up and walked out of the room, and when he came back in he was holding his gun. "I got beef with that nigga, too" he said, bending over her. "When I'm done, you gonna be marrying me. You'll be going with me to New York because I'm gonna take over that nigga's work, which I had my eye on for a long time. And when I met you, that made it even easier for me."

Kanika managed to sit up and get out of the bed. She held on to the wall. "Saliq, you really fucked up on this one. If you think I'd ever do anything with you, you are sicker than you look." She shot a wad of spit in his eye.

The saliva ran down his face. He didn't even wipe it off but glared at her. "Your father been good to me, but I'm never going to rule if I stay here in VA."

"That's *your* fucking problem," Kanika said, inching her way around him. "I'm getting the hell outta here."

Saliq grabbed her long hair and dragged her back toward the bed. He picked her up again, threw her on the bed, and ripped her blouse open. He unsnapped her bra and fondled her breasts roughly, making them hurt. He licked them wildly as Kanika tried to squirm her way from underneath him. She could barely move her legs, not to mention her entire body enough to flee.

"Keep that ass still," he said. "I told you. I didn't get to come." His tongue felt wet and slimy across her ears. She wished she had a gun to blow his brains out. All she could do was lie there under his weight. Even if she had to bite his tongue off, she wasn't going to let him get inside her panties again.

Saliq held Kanika down while she kicked and screamed. "I'm just waiting for your ass to get tired."

Kanika scratched his face several times, but Saliq went about his business ravaging her body with his dick. Saliq dug his dick in her dry pussy.

"No, no!" Kanika fought, but to no avail. She stared at the ceiling as Saliq devastated her with painful, vicious thrusts while he held her down. All she could see was his eyes rolling back into his head and the sweat forming around his face and neck. He was crazy and she was, too, for ever thinking she could be with this man. As Saliq came on her stomach, it was the first time in her life that she wished she were dead since Waleema's death.

"Call Tyrell and tell him to meet you somewhere so I can cap his ass, or I'm gonna tear this pussy up so bad this time, you gonna need stitches," he said, his nails digging into its delicate flesh. Kanika tried not to scream. "Get on the phone!" he said, shoving his cell into her face. But she refused.

Trembling, Kanika couldn't compose herself to talk.

"Fuck it," he muttered, wiping his dick off with the bedsheet.

"Wait till Daddy finds out about this, Saliq," Kanika cried.

"Your daddy ain't gonna do shit," Saliq said, turning away from. But just then his cell phone rang. He snatched it up. "Yo."

"I got that nigga Tyrell over here and I'm about to do him up nice," Shon said, not bothering to identify himself. His voice was cold, deadly. "I want you over here in less than ten to deal with this shit."

Saliq looked at Kanika out the corner of his eye, a half-smile curving his lips. This couldn't have worked out more perfectly. "So Mr. New York is down here in VA, huh, Shon?" He watched Kanika's eyes widen in horror. She tried to rise up off the bed once again, but Saliq quickly grabbed her by the throat and slammed her back down. He smiled as she fought him. "You know I got beef with that mothafucka myself."

No, no, no! Kanika thought frantically, dark spots beginning to dance in front of her eyes.

"You know Kanika is here with me." she heard Saliq say. There was a brief pause, then Saliq laughed. "Sounds good. We'll be there." He hung up his cell phone and tossed it on the bed.

"Well, bitch," he said, leaning down into her face. "Seems like your baby boy is a dead man and your daddy wants you to have a front row seat. Apparently there's some things you need to know about your man before he dies."

"Fuck . . . you!" Kanika gasped.

An ugly expression came over Saliq's face and his fingers began to slowly tighten around her throat. It wasn't long before Kanika slipped down into darkness.

Thirty

"Yo, Shon!" Saliq said, as he barged past Tiffany and into the house, carrying an unconscious Kanika in his arms.

"He downstairs in the Crypt," Tiffany said, referring to the subbasement of the house. She didn't even look twice at Kanika. "Why don't you put that bitch down for a minute and let's get a quickie in before she wakes up?"

The Crypt was a small enclave her father built when he bought the house as a secret hideout where he handled some of his deadliest deals. With Tyrell downstairs with him, Saliq thought that he may have missed out on the best part already and decided to have some fun with Tiffany. He laid Kanika's limp body down on the sofa, grabbed Tiffany by her fleshy arm, and said, "Get on your knees in the corner ova' there."

Saliq was full of adrenaline. He studied Tiffany's

imperfect body as she crawled, half-naked, to a nook under the staircase. He lifted up her skirt farther, pulled out his dick, and slammed into her ass.

"Owww, that shit hurt!" Tiffany frowned, not expecting him to go that route. She'd had anal sex several times, and usually after a few minutes she'd enjoyed the feeling.

But Saliq pounded into her ass hard enough that she began to bleed. He closed his eyes and bit down on his teeth as he busted inside of Tiffany. He gripped her breasts, squeezing them between his fingers. Leaning over to bite her shoulders, he stuck his fingers down her throat.

"Saliq!" Tiffany squealed, fighting the choking sensation. She gagged a few times, with coats of spit covering his fingers, but he didn't let up. It wasn't until he caught himself that he stopped. It was like something had come over him. He felt out of control and he liked every minute of it.

When he was through, he pushed Tiffany to the side. "Don't you tell your fuckin' father about this shit. You *made* me do this. Remember that," he warned.

Tiffany nodded. It wasn't the first time they'd had sex, because she had been giving Saliq some since she was fifteen and he was twenty-one. She just hoped that one day he'd want to have more of her than just a piece of ass.

While Tiffany scurried up the steps to tend to her battered body, Saliq thought it was time to attend to his business. Kanika was still unconscious. He thought there was no better evidence to complement the story he was about to give her father.

Saliq descended the long steps to the Crypt with Kanika's body in his arms. He pressed his combination and opened the cold, steel door. Shon was seated on a long chrome steel couch draped in a gold velvet throw and pillows. He was facing the door, and Tyrell was seated across from him with his hands and feet tied.

"Yo, you won't believe what happened," Saliq said, faking a grin.

Shon calmly approached him and Kanika, felt her pulse, and said, "She'll be fine."

Tyrell could barely move when he saw Kanika's seemingly lifeless arms and legs. "Kanika!" he said, struggling against his ropes. "What da fuck do you mean, she'll be fine? Her face is nearly white, yo."

"She probably got in the way of some man business. Hard time minding her business, just like her mama," Shon said, taking Kanika from Saliq's arms. He placed her on the couch.

But Saliq had all his attention focused on Tyrell. "So you that nigga?"

"Yeah, motherfucka! And you gonna be that dead nigga!" Tyrell said with a distorted grin that looked like he couldn't wait for the shit to drop.

Saliq folded his arms and said to Shon, "She came up to my crib, wanting to get a little physical and all that. When I told her I wasn't interested and that I was gonna tell you about how she was acting, she went crazy on me, threw herself down the steps, and got knocked out."

Shon laughed. "The apple doesn't fall far from the tree."

"Yo, get me out of this shit. She needs to be woken up or she can die," Tyrell said to Shon, who hesitantly untied him.

"You a lyin' piece of shit" Tyrell said. "Nika don't act like that. Kanika would never try to hurt herself!"

As Saliq and her father stood by, Tyrell kissed Kanika's lips, her hands, until she threw her eyes open. She clutched Tyrell's hands. "I thought I was dreaming. I was in the bed, and," Kanika felt her neck, "I was being choked and then—"

All of a sudden Kanika gave a little moan, her hands coming up as if she were fighting someone off. Her eyes flew open with a gasp. She immediately turned on her side and began to cough violently. Shon stroked her back. Finally she fell back on the couch and tried to catch her breath. Shon went over to another chair, crossed his legs, and lit one of his cigars.

Eventually, Kanika got herself together long enough to sit up and look around. She froze when she saw where they were, and Tyrell staring at her like a starving man, gazing upon his last feast.

It was a shock to see him and she felt as if all the breath were being squeezed out of her once again.

He was so handsome. There was nothing she wanted more in that moment than to run to him. Her eyes filled with tears. There was still nothing in this world that she wanted more than him.

"Glad you could join us, baby," Shon said, calmly.

Kanika looked over at him, then to Tyrell and Saliq, and knew that one of her worst nightmares had come to life. She carefully swung her legs around so that her feet were now touching the floor. She looked at Saliq, who stared back at her, daring her to say something about what had happened.

Motherfucker, she thought.

She studied Shon. He looked laid-back, but she could see the deadly cold in his eyes and knew that he was in a killing mood. She was going to have to keep her head and be *real careful* now.

"Daddy," she said, "what's Tyrell doing here?"

"Now, that's an interesting story, baby," he said, puffing on his cigar. He tilted his head back and blew a smoke ring up at the ceiling.

"Maybe Tyrell can help me out. What do you think, Tyrell?"

Kanika looked at him. "What is it?"

Tyrell's eyes welled up. He just couldn't tell her like this. He had planned to tell her everything in privacy, when they had their own family, when she couldn't just leave him—one day.

"It's about Waleema. About how you killed her?" Shon said, nodding. "Go ahead."

Kanika peered into Tyrell's eyes. "What?" she whispered.

Tyrell realized that the moment had come. There was no way to sugarcoat this, he thought. He took in a long deep breath and began, "I told you about Tony. Niggas wanted him out after he killed Cee-Lo. I had to take him out, or we all would of went down. He was going to get *you* killed and I couldn't let that happen. I couldn't, Kanika. Hired some mother-fuckas and they did that shit. But—"

Tyrell lost his train of thought at the look in Kanika's eyes. It was as if she'd seen a ghost. That love, admiration, that dream, that used to be in her eyes for him was really gone. He wanted her to slap him, spit at him, or whatever, just to get it out. But Kanika was frozen in shock.

He forced himself to go on. "They ended up at the right place, but at the wrong time. Tony told me he was gonna be at his office that night. That you and your mama had plans that day. And that was why I told you I couldn't see you that day. You and your mama was there when the shooting went down and got caught up, Kanika. If you wanna kill me right here and now, do it. I don't think I could live with losing your mama, and losing you."

No one can kill like this nigga can, she thought in some far-off part of her brain. She was too shocked to feel anything. Disbelief, anger, or pain. She was numb, she was done, she was dead inside, and her one true love had slaughtered her in so many ways.

She stared at him, slowly shaking her head. "You killed the only person who ever loved me," she said, her eyes filling with tears. The pain was starting to bloom, fast. The fury, she knew, would follow.

Shon put his cigar between his teeth, stood up, reached behind him, and pulled out a .45. He walked over to Kanika and placed the .45 in her limp hand. He curled her fingers around it. "Baby, show this nigga how it's done," he said, his voice now raw. She looked up at him and saw the rage in his eyes. "Just like your mama would."

Tyrell didn't move or say anything else in his defense. He just continued to look at Kanika. No matter what was about to go down, he would always love her. He understood her position and wished he could shoot himself for her.

Kanika gripped the gun, cocked the hammer, and leveled the gun at Tyrell's face. She thought about shooting him right between the eyes. She wanted him to feel the same pain her mother felt with a bullet in her skull. Kanika's finger trembled on the trigger. She thought about her own life.

"Just shoot that motherfucka!" Shon said, positioning the gun more securely in her hand.

Kanika and Tyrell's gazes consumed each other. Even as she looked at him, she didn't see the evil in him that he had admitted to. Tyrell was a lost soul. She had always known it, even when she had first met him when she was only twelve years old. She realized now that even then, she had wanted to save him. To answer that desperate plea in his eyes. That look in his eyes that asked if he could be saved, if he would ever be worthy. That was what drove him to church every Sunday. He was in search of that answer. He also wanted so much, was determined to have it all, including her, but deep down, he didn't believe that he deserved it. Tony had been like the father Tyrell didn't have, and she didn't doubt that he had loved Tony deeply and that it had killed some part of his spirit to take him down. She also knew that he loved the life that he had created when he hooked up with Tony and that was why he had done it—to protect that life at all costs. For the first time in his life, Tyrell belonged somewhere and had people and a place that he could call his own. That was worth the world to him. She had been the jewel in that crown, the final piece that he had been missing. And he had probably been right. She knew that Tony had been making a bad situation even worse. She knew that the streets had been hot and that rumors had been flying, even while Waleema had told her to mind her own business. But it was his guilt that caused him to destroy what he had now, even while he had it all in the palm of his hand. He hadn't slept with Peaches because he wanted her. He had slept with Peaches because sleeping with his girl's best friend was the kind of thing that a man who would kill his father would do.

She knew that Tyrell had loved her mother and that he had never meant for Waleema to die. She also knew that he loved her more than his own life. Besides her mother, he was the only one to love her unconditionally. On the flip side, her father's love always came with conditions and stipulations. Even now, he wanted her to shoot Tyrell, not to avenge her mother, but to prove her loyalty to him and his brand of justice. But she could not kill this man. She understood him and everything that drove him. And she loved and hated him for it. She let her arm drop to her side.

"I can't do it," she told Shon.

"Bitch!" Saliq shouted. "I knew you wouldn't do it." He raised his gun at Tyrell and squeezed the trigger.

Kanika screamed, swung the gun up, and fired. She kept squeezing the trigger until she had no bullets left. Saliq lay on the ground, riddled with bullets, his gun flung away from his body.

Shon stared down at Saliq, his cigar now dangling limply from his lips. He looked up at Kanika, and she began to shake at the look in his eyes. He spit the cigar out, raised his gun, and said, "Damn it, baby girl." And fired.

Tyrell dove for Kanika, knocking her to the ground. Then he rolled, snatched up Saliq's gun, turned, and fired at her father, hitting right between the eyes. Shon fell to the ground with that mask of fury still etched into his face.

Tyrell grabbed Kanika and the guns and got the hell out of the house. Neither knew where Tiffany was or if she had called the cops. But as they drove away, Kanika saw Tiffany looking stone-faced at them from the window. Kanika wondered if their nightmare had ended or just begun.

Thirty-one

Thirty-one

Tyrell raced up the highway, trying to put as much
distance as possible between them and the ugly
scene he and Kanika had just left behind.

"Don't worry, yo," he said, his gaze fixed intensely on the road. He glanced at Kanika out the
corner of his eye. She looked like she was still in
shock. "It's gonna be all right. I'm going to take
care of this, Kanika. Of you. I'm never gonna let no
shit like what just went down happen to you again."

Kanika couldn't believe that Saliq and her father
were dead. She'd pull the trigger and ice that nigger
Saliq all over again if she had to, but she couldn't
believe that everything had gone down the way it
had gone down. She took a deep breath. Everything
was going to change now. She looked at Tyrell. And
some things hadn't changed at all.

"Pull the car over, Tyrell."

He looked at her in surprise. "What? What the hell

you talking about Kanika? We gotta get out of here, back to New York where I can protect you, baby."

Kanika shook her head. "No, you don't. I'm not yours to protect anymore, remember?"

Tyrell got real quiet and his hands gripped the steering wheel. All of a sudden he jerked the steering wheel to the right. Kanika heard the angry blare of horns and the screech of tires and grabbed the door handle and held on. Tyrell brought the car to a stop when he reached the shoulder. He shut the car off and turned to face her.

"Nigga, what the hell do you think you're doing?" Kanika asked, her tone excited. She put a hand over her pounding heart.

"Kanika," he said, "I came down her to get you back, and I ain't leavin' without you."

Kanika let her hand drop to her lap. "You don't have a choice, Tyrell. What just happened with Saliq and my father doesn't change anything between us. You still slept with my best friend. How am I supposed to trust you again, Tyrell?" Tears filled her eyes. All of a sudden she felt overwhelmed by it all. Her mother was dead, Tony was dead, her father had tried to kill Tyrell and her, she had killed Saliq, Tyrell had killed her father. She put her head in her hands and began to cry. It wasn't supposed to be like this. She was a ghetto princess and Tyrell was supposed to be her ghetto prince and they were supposed to be ruling over their hood kingdom together. Instead, everything had turned to shit and she didn't know how she was going to pick up the pieces.

Tyrell grabbed her and folded her in his arms. "I promise, it will be different this time, Nika." His voice shook as well. He held her so tight, she almost couldn't breathe. "I will never hurt you like that again. Never. You're my life, Nika. Can't nobody take your place in my heart."

For a moment, Kanika just closed her eyes and let Tyrell soak up her tears, her pain. It felt so good to be in his arms again, to feel his body next to hers. She slid her arms around him and just held on. She buried her nose in his neck. No one smelled like Tyrell. She pulled back from him, then leaned in once again, kissed him, and got lost all over again.

When Tyrell let go of her, she stared up into his eyes and said, "I'm sorry, Tyrell. But it's over."

Tyrell let go of her. He leaned back against the car door and they just stared at each other.

"You'll never forgive me for what happened to Tony and your mother," he said, finally.

Kanika shook her head. "No, I forgive you for that, Tyrell. The pain will never go away, but I understand why you made the decision you made. I know you loved Tony and tried everything else. And I don't think that you ever meant for Mommy to get hurt." She looked down at her lap. "I think I even understand what happened with Peaches—or at least why." She looked back up at him. "You need to forgive yourself, Tyrell, or you're going to lose everything . . . the way you lost me."

Tyrell closed his eyes and for a long time said nothing. Then he finally faced forward, turned on the car, and pulled back onto the road. "Where to?" he asked.

"Take me back home."

His head whipped around. *"What?"*

"I have to go back, Tyrell, or the cops are going to think I did it. And who the hell knows what that bitch, Tiffany, is going to feed them."

"You are responsible, Kanika," Tyrell said. "You shot that nigga dead."

"You got the guns, so they won't know that. As long as you get rid of them, both of us should be all right."

Tyrell shook his head. "That's some risky shit, Kanika."

"I run, I look like I'm guilty. I'm going home, Tyrell, and I'm going to handle it."

Tyrell didn't say anything, but he took her back home. He stopped the car about five houses down from hers. The neighborhood looked as peaceful as ever. It looked like a bloody shootout had never happened in one of their rich homes.

Looks like Tiffany just got the fuck out of dodge, Kanika thought to herself. *I'll be ready for that bitch when she comes back up.* In the meantime, she had to call the cops and spin them a bedtime story. She put her hand on the door handle. She hesitated. "Good-bye, Tyrell."

Tyrell reached out and grabbed her arm. "It isn't over between us, baby. I always knew you were meant to be my wifey and that hasn't changed. I fucked things up, but I'm going to get you back. Just think about that while you down here, handling your business." His thumb brushed her cheek. "Ghetto princess."

Kanika pushed the car door open and ran to her father's house. No, it probably wasn't over between them. Tyrell would make sure of that.